BY

AUSTIN CRAIG

Contents

DEDICATION

To the Philippine Youth

The subject of Doctor Rizal's first prizewinning poem was The Philippine Youth, and its theme was "Growth." The study of the growth of free ideas, as illustrated in this book of his lineage, life and labors, may therefore fittingly be dedicated to the "fair hope of the fatherland."

Except in the case of some few men of great genius, those who are accustomed to absolutism cannot comprehend democracy. Therefore our nation is relying on its young men and young women; on the rising, instructed generation, for the secure establishment of popular selfgovernment in the Philippines. This was Rizal's own idea, for he said, through the old philosopher in "Noli me Tangere," that he was not writing for his own generation but for a coming, instructed generation that would understand his hidden meaning.

Your public school education gives you the democratic view-point, which the genius of Rizal gave him; in the fifty-five volumes of the BlairRobertson translation of Philippine historical material there is available today more about your country's past than the entire contents of the British Museum afforded him; and you have the guidance in the new paths that Rizal struck out, of the life of a hero who, farsightedly or providentially, as you may later decide, was the forerunner of the present régime.

But you will do as he would have done, neither accept anything because it is written, nor reject it because it does not fall in with your prejudices—study out the truth for yourselves.

Introduction

In writing a biography, the author, if he be discriminating, selects, with great care, the salient features of the life story of the one whom he deems worthy of being portrayed as a person possessed of preëminent qualities that make for a character and greatness. Indeed to write biography at all, one should have that nice sense of proportion that makes him instinctively seize upon only those points that do advance his theme. Boswell has given the world an example of biography that is often wearisome in the extreme, although he wrote about a man who occupied in his time a commanding position. Because Johnson was Johnson the world accepts Boswell, and loves to talk of the minuteness of Boswell's portrayal, yet how many read him, or if they do read him, have the patience to read him to the end?

In writing the life of the greatest of the Filipinos, Mr. Craig has displayed judgment. Saturated as he is with endless details of Rizal's life, he has had the good taste to select those incidents or those phases of Rizal's life that exhibit his greatness of soul and that show the factors that were the most potent in shaping his character and in controlling his purposes and actions.

A biography written with this chastening of wealth cannot fail to be instructive and worthy of study. If one were to point out but a single benefit that can accrue from a study of biography written as Mr. Craig has done that of Rizal, he would mention, I believe, that to the character of the student, for one cannot study seriously about men of character without being affected by that study. As leading to an understanding of the character of Rizal, Mr. Craig has described his ancestry with considerable fulness and has shown how the selective principle has worked through successive generations. But he has also realized the value of the outside influences and shows how the accidents of birth and nation affected by environment plus mental vigor and will produced José Rizal. With a strikingly meager setting of detail, Rizal has been portrayed from every side and the reader must leave the biography with a knowledge of the elements that entered into and made his life. As a study for the youth of the

Philippines, I believe this life of Rizal will be productive of good results. Stimulation and purpose are presented (yet not didactically) throughout its pages. One object of the author, I should say, has been to show how both Philippine history and world history helped shape Rizal's character. Accordingly, he has mentioned many historical matters both of Philippine and world-wide interest. One cannot read the book without a desire to know more of these matters. Thus the book is not only a biography, it is a history as well. It must give a larger outlook to the youth of the Philippines. The only drawback that one might find in it, and it seems paradoxical to say it, is the lack of more detail, for one leaves it wishing that he knew more of the actual intimate happenings, and this, I take it, is the best effect a biography can have on the reader outside of the instructive and moral value of the biography.

JAMES A. ROBERTSON.

MANILA, P. I.

CONTENTS

LIST OF ILLUSTRATIONS

Philippine Money and Postage Stamps

Portrait of Rizal
Painted in oils by Juan Luna in Paris. Facsimile (in color).

Columbus at Barcelona
From a print in Rizal's scrapbook.

Portrait Group Rizal at thirteen. Rizal at eighteen. Rizal in London. The portrait on the postage stamp.

The Baptismal Record of Domingo Lam-co Facsimile.

Portrait Group 1. In Luna's home. 2. In 1890. 3. The portrait on the paper money. 4. In 1891. 5. In 1892.

Pacific Ocean Spheres of Influence Made by Rizal during President Harrison's administration.

Father of Rizal Portrait.

Mother of Rizal Portrait.

Rizal's Family-Tree
Made by Rizal when in Dapitan.

Birthplace of José Rizal From a photograph.

Sketches by Rizal
A group made during his travels.

Bust of Rizal's Father Carved in wood by Rizal.

The Church and Convento at Kalamba From a photograph.

Father Leoncio Lopez From a photograph.

The Lake District of Central Luzon Sketch made by Rizal.

The Story of the Monkey and the Tortoise Six facsimiles from Rizal's originals.

CHAPTER I

America's Forerunner

THE lineage of a hero who made the history of his country during its most critical period, and whose labors constitute its hope for the future, must be more than a simple list of an ascending line. The blood which flowed in his veins must be traced generation by generation, the better to understand the man, but at the same time the causes leading to the conditions of his times must be noted, step by step, in order to give a better understanding of the environment in which he lived and labored.

The study of the growth of free ideas is now in the days of our democracy the most important feature of Philippine history; hitherto this history has consisted of little more than lists of governors, their term of office, and of the recital of such incidents as were considered to redound to the glory of Spain, or could be so twisted and misrepresented as to make them appear to do so. It rarely occurred to former historians that the lamp of experience might prove a light for the feet of future generations, and the mistakes of the past were usually ignored or passed over, thus leaving the way open for repeating the old errors. But profit, not pride, should be the object of the study of the past, and our historians of today very largely concern themselves with mistakes in policy and defects of system; fortunately for them such critical investigation under our changed conditions does not involve the discomfort and danger that attended it in the days of Doctor Rizal.

In the opinion of the martyred Doctor, criticism of the right sort—even the very best things may be abused till they become intolerable evils—serves much the same useful warning purpose for governments that the symptoms of sickness do for persons. Thus government and individual alike, when advised in time of something wrong with the system, can seek out and correct the cause before serious consequences ensue. But the nation that represses honest criticism with severity, like the individual who deadens his symptoms with dangerous drugs, is likely to be lulled into a false security that may prove fatal. Patriot toward Spain and the Philippines alike, Rizal tried to impress this view upon the government of his day, with fatal results to himself, and the disastrous effects of not heeding him have since justified his position.

The very defenses of Old Manila illustrate how the Philippines have suffered from lack of such devoted, honest and courageous critics as José Rizal. The city wall was built some years later than the first Spanish occupation to keep out Chinese pirates after Li Ma-hong destroyed the city. The Spaniards sheltered themselves in the old Tagalog fort till reënforcements could come from the country. No one had ever dared to quote the proverb about locking the door after the horse was stolen. The need for the moat, so recently filled in, was not seen until after the bitter experience of the easy occupation of Manila by the English, but if public opinion had been allowed free expression this experience might have been avoided. And the free space about the walls was cleared of buildings only after these same buildings had helped to make the same occupation of the city easier, yet there were many in Manila who foresaw the danger but feared to foretell it.

Had the people of Spain been free to criticise the Spaniards' way of waiting to do things until it is too late, that nation, at one time the largest and richest empire in the world, would probably have been saved from its loss of territory and its present impoverished condition. And had the early Filipinos, to whom splendid professions and sweeping promises were made, dared to complain of the Peninsular policy of procrastination—the "mañana" habit, as it has been called—Spain might have been spared Doctor Rizal's terrible but true indictment that she retarded Philippine progress, kept the Islands miserably ruled for 333 years and in the last days of the nineteenth century was still permitting mediaeval malpractices. Rizal did not believe that his country was able to stand alone as a separate government. He therefore desired to preserve the Spanish sovereignty in the Philippines, but he desired also to bring about reforms and conditions conducive to advancement. To this end he carefully pointed out those colonial shortcomings that caused friction, kept up discontent, and prevented safe progress, and that would have been perfectly easy to correct. Directly as well as indirectly, the changes he proposed were calculated to benefit the homeland quite as much as the Philippines, but his wellmeaning efforts brought him hatred and an undeserved death, thus proving once more how thankless is the task of telling unpleasant truths, no matter how necessary it may be to do so. Because Rizal spoke out boldly, while realizing what would probably be his fate, history holds him a hero and calls his death a martyrdom. He was not one of those popularity-seeking, self-styled patriots who are ever mouthing "My country, right or wrong;" his devotion was deeper and more disinterested. When he found his country wrong he willingly sacrificed himself to set her right. Such unselfish spirits are rare; in life they are often misunderstood, but when time does them justice, they come into a fame which endures.

Doctor Rizal knew that the real Spain had generous though sluggish intentions, and noble though erratic impulses, but it awoke too late; too late for Doctor Rizal and too late to save the Philippines for Spain; tardy reforms after his death were useless and the loss of her overseas possessions was the result. Doctor Rizal lost when he staked his life on his trust in the innate sense of honor of Spain, for that sense of honor became temporarily blinded by a sudden but fatal gust of passion; and it took the shock of the separation to rouse the dormant Spanish chivalry.

Still in the main Rizal's judgment was correct, and he was the victim of mistimed, rather than of misplaced, confidence, for as soon as the knowledge of the real Rizal became known to the Spanish people, belated justice began to be done his memory, and then, repentant and remorseful, as is characteristically Castilian, there was little delay and no half-heartedness. Another name may now be grouped with Columbus and Cervantes among those to whom Spain has given imprisonment in life and monuments after death—chains for the man and chaplets for his memory. In 1896, during the few days before he could be returned to Manila, Doctor Rizal occupied a dungeon in Montjuich Castle in Barcelona; while on his way to assist the Spanish soldiers in Cuba who were stricken with yellow fever, he was shipped and sent back to a prejudged trial and an unjust execution. Fifteen years later the Catalan city authorities commemorated the semi-centennial of this prisoner's birth by changing, in his honor, the name of a street in the shadow of the infamous prison of Montjuich Castle to "Calle del Doctor Rizal." More instances of this nature are not cited since they are not essential to the proper understanding of Rizal's story, but let it be made clear once for all that whatever harshness may be found in the following pages is directed solely to those who betrayed the trust of the mother country and

selfishly abused the ample and unrestrained powers with which Spain invested them.

And what may seem the exaltation of the Anglo-Saxons at the expense of the Latins in these pages is intended only to point out the superiority of their ordered system of government, with its checks and balances, its individual rights and individual duties, under which men are "free to live by no man's leave, underneath the Law." No human being can be safely trusted with unlimited power, and no man, no matter what his nationality, could have withstood the temptations offered by the chaotic conditions in the Philippines in past times any better than did the Spaniards. There is nothing written in this book that should convey the opinion that in similar circumstances men of any nationality would not have acted as the Spaniards did. The easiest recognized characteristic of absolutism, and all the abuses and corruption
it brings in its train, is fear of criticism, and Spain drew her own indictment in the Philippines when she executed Rizal.

When any nation sets out to enroll all its scholarly critics among the martyrs in the cause of Liberty, it makes an open confession of guilt to all the world. For a quarter of a century Spain had been ruling in the Philippines by terrorizing its subjects there, and Rizal's execution, with utter disregard of the most elementary rules of judicial procedure, was the culmination that drove the Filipinos to desperation and arrested the attention of the whole civilized world. It was evident that Rizal's fate might have been that of any of his countrymen, and the thinking world saw that events had taken such a course in the Philippines that it had become justifiable for the Filipinos to attempt to dissolve the political bands which had connected them with Spain for over three centuries.

Such action by the Filipinos would not have been warranted by a solitary instance of unjust execution under stress of political excitement that did not indicate the existence of a settled policy. Such instances are rather to be classed among the mistakes to which governments as well as individuals are liable. Yet even such a mistake may be avoided by certain precautions which experience has suggested, and the nation that disregards these precautions is justly open to criticism.

Our present Philippine government guarantees to its citizens as fundamental rights, that no person shall be held to answer for a capital crime unless on an indictment, nor may he be compelled in any criminal case to be a witness against himself, nor be deprived of life, liberty or property without due process of law. The accused must have a speedy, public and impartial trial, be informed of the nature and cause of the accusation, be confronted with the witnesses against him, have compulsory process for obtaining witnesses in his favor, and have the assistance of counsel for his defense. Not one of these safeguards protected Doctor Rizal except that he had an "open trial," if that name may be given to a courtroom filled with his enemies openly clamoring for his death without rebuke from the court. Even the presumption of innocence till guilt was established was denied him. These precautions have been considered necessary for every criminal trial, but the framers of the American Constitution, fearful lest popular prejudice some day might cause injustice to those advocating unpopular ideals, prohibited the irremediable penalty of death upon a charge of treason except where the testimony of two reliable witnesses established some overt act, inference not being admissible as evidence.

Such protection was not given the subjects of

Spain, but still, with all the laxity of the Spanish law, and even if all the charges had been true, which they were far from being, no case was made out against Doctor Rizal at his trial. According to the laws then in effect, he was unfairly convicted and he should be considered innocent; for this reason his life will be studied to see what kind of hero he was, and no attempt need be made to plead good character and honest intentions in extenuation of illegal acts. Rizal was ever the advocate of law, and it will be found, too, that he was always consistently lawabiding.

Though they are in the Orient, the Filipinos are not of it. Rizal once said, upon hearing of plans for a Philippine exhibit at a European World's Fair, that the people of Europe would have a chance to see themselves as they were in the Middle Ages. With allowances for the changes due to climate and for the character of the country, this statement can hardly be called exaggerated. The Filipinos in the last half of the nineteenth century were not Orientals but mediaeval Europeans—to the credit of the early Castilians but to the discredit of the later Spaniards.

The Filipinos of the remoter Christian barrios, whom Rizal had in mind particularly, were in customs, beliefs and advancement substantially what the descendants of Legaspi's followers might have been had these been shipwrecked on the sparsely inhabited islands of the Archipelago and had their settlement remained shut off from the rest of the world.

Except where foreign influence had accidentally crept in at the ports, it could truthfully be said that scarcely perceptible advance had been made in three hundred years. Succeeding Spaniards by their misrule not only added little to the glorious achievement of their ancestors, but seemed to have prevented the natural progress which the land would have made.

In one form or another, this contention was the basis of Rizal's campaign. By careful search, it is true, isolated instances of improvement could be found, but the showing at its very best was so pitifully poor that the system stood discredited. And it was the system to which Rizal was opposed.

The Spaniards who engaged in public argument with Rizal were continually discovering, too late to avoid tumbling into them, logical pitfalls which had been carefully prepared to trap them. Rizal argued much as he played chess, and was ever ready to sacrifice a pawn to be enabled to say "check." Many an unwary opponent realized after he had published what he had considered a clever answer that the same reasoning which scored a point against Rizal incontrovertibly established the Kalamban's major premise.

Superficial antagonists, to the detriment of their own reputations, have made much of what they chose to consider Rizal's historical errors. But history is not merely chronology, and his representation of its trend, disregarding details, was a masterly tracing of current evils to their remote causes. He may have erred in some of his minor statements; this will happen to anyone who writes much, but attempts to discredit Rizal on the score of historical inaccuracy really reflect upon the captious critics, just as a draftsman would expose himself to ridicule were he to complain of some famous historical painting that it had not been drawn to exact scale.

Rizal's writings were intended to bring out in relief the evils of the Spanish system of the government of the Filipino people, just as a map of the world may put the inhabited portions of the earth in greater prominence than those portions that are not inhabited. Neither is exact in its representation, but each serves its purpose the better because it magnifies the important and minimizes the unimportant.

In his disunited and abased countrymen, Rizal's writings aroused, as he intended they should, the spirit of nationality, of a Fatherland which was not Spain, and put their feet on the road to progress. What matters it, then, if his historical references are not always exhaustive, and if to make himself intelligible in the Philippines he had to write in a style possibly not always sanctioned by the Spanish Academy? Spain herself had denied to the Filipinos a system of education that might have made a creditable Castilian the common language of the Archipelago. A display of erudition alone does not make an historian, nor is purity, propriety and precision in choosing words all there is to literature.

Rizal charged Spain unceasingly with unprogressiveness in the Philippines, just as he labored and planned unwearyingly to bring the Filipinos abreast of modern European civilization. But in his appeals to the Spanish conscience and in his endeavors to educate his countrymen he showed himself as practical as he was in his arguments, ever ready to concede nonessentials in name and means if by doing so progress could be made.

Because of his unceasing efforts for a wiser, better governed and more prosperous Philippines, and because of his frank admission that he hoped thus in time there might come a freer Philippines, Rizal was called traitor to Spain and ingrate. Now honest, open criticism is not treason, and the sincerest gratitude to those who first brought Christian civilization to the Philippines should not shut the eyes to the wrongs which Filipinos suffered from their successors. But until the latest moment of Spanish rule, the apologists of Spain seemed to think that they ought to be able to turn away the wrath evoked by the cruelty and incompetence that ran riot during centuries, by dwelling upon the benefits of the early days of the Spanish dominion.

Wearisome was the eternal harping on gratitude which at one time was the only safe tone for pulpit, press and public speech; it irritating because it ignored questions of current policy, and it was discouraging to the Filipinos who were reminded by it of the hopeless future for their country to which time had brought no progress. But with all the faults and unworthiness of the later rulers, and the inane attempts of their parasites to distract attention from these failings, there remains undimmed the luster of Spain's early fame. The Christianizing which accompanied her flag upon the mainland and islands of the New World is its imperishable glory, and the transformation of the Filipino people from Orientals into mediæval Europeans through the colonizing genius of the early Castilians, remains a marvel unmatched in colonial history and merits the lasting gratitude of the Filipino.

Doctor Rizal satirized the degenerate descendants and scored the unworthy successors, but his writings may be searched in vain for wholesale charges against the Spanish nation such as Spanish scribblers were forever directing against all Filipinos, past, present and future, with an alleged fault of a single one as a pretext. It will be found that he invariably recognized that the faithful first administrators and the devoted pioneer missionaries had a valid claim upon the continuing gratitude of the people of Tupa's and Lakandola's land.

Rizal's insight discerned, and experience has demonstrated, that Legaspi, Urdaneta and those who were like them, laid broad and firm foundations for a modern social and political organization which could be safely and speedily established by reforms from above. The early Christianizing civilizers deserve no part of the blame for the fact that Philippine ports were not earlier opened to progress, but much credit is due them that there is succeeding here an orderly democracy such as now would be impossible in any neighboring country.

The Philippine patriot would be the first to recognize the justice of the selection of portraits which appear with that of Rizal upon the present Philippine postage stamps, where they serve as daily reminders of how free government came here.

The constancy and courage of a Portuguese sailor put these Islands into touch with the New World with which their future progress was to be identified. The tact and honesty of a civil official from Mexico made possible the almost bloodless conquest which brought the Filipinos under the then helpful rule of Spain. The bequest of a far-sighted early philanthropist was the beginning of the water system of Manila, which was a recognition of the importance of efforts toward improving the public health and remains a reminder of how, even in the darkest days of miseries and misgovernment, there have not been wanting Spaniards whose ideal of Spanish patriotism was to devote heart, brain and wealth to the welfare of the Filipinos. These were the heroes of the period of preparation.

The life of the one whose story is told in these pages was devoted and finally sacrificed to dignify their common country in the eyes of his countrymen, and to unite them in a common patriotism; he inculcated that self-respect which, by leading to self-restraint and self-control, makes self-government possible; and sought to inspire in all a love of ordered freedom, so that, whether under the flag of Spain or any other, or by themselves, neither tyrants (caciques) nor slaves (those led by caciques) would be possible among them.

And the change itself came through an American President who believed, and practiced the belief, that nations owed obligations to other nations just as men had duties toward their fellow-men. He established here Liberty through Law, and provided for progress in general education, which should be a safeguard to good government as well, for an enlightened people cannot be an oppressed people. Then he went to war against the Philippines rather than deceive them, because the Filipinos, who repeatedly had been tricked by Spain with unfulfilled promises, insisted on pledges which he had not the power to give. They knew nothing of what was meant by the rule of the people, and could not conceive of a government whose head was the servant and not the master. Nor did they realize that even the voters might not promise for the future, since republicanism requires that the government of any period shall rule only during the period that it is in the majority. In that war military glory and quick conquest were sacrificed to consideration for the misled enemy, and every effort was made to minimize the evils of warfare and to gain the confidence of the people. Retaliation for violations of the usages of civilized warfare, of which Filipinos at first were guilty through their Spanish training, could not be entirely prevented, but this retaliation contrasted strikingly with the Filipinos' unhappy past experiences with Spanish soldiers. The few who had been educated out of Spain and therefore understood the American position were daily reënforced by those persons who became convinced from what they saw, until a majority of the Philippine people sought peace. Then the President of the United States outlined a policy, and the history and constitution of his government was an assurance that this policy would be followed; the American government then began to do what it had not been able to promise.

The forerunner and the founder of the present regime in these Islands, by a strange coincidence, were as alike in being cruelly misunderstood in their lifetimes by those whom they sought to benefit as they were in the tragedy of their deaths, and both were unjustly judged by many, probably wellmeaning, countrymen.

Magellan, Legaspi, Carriedo, Rizal and McKinley, heroes of the free Philippines, belonged to different times and were of different types, but their work combined to make possible the growing democracy of today. The diversity of nationalities among these heroes is an added advantage, for it recalls that mingling of blood which has developed the Filipinos into a strong people.

England, the United States and the Philippines are each composed of widely diverse elements. They have each been developed by adversity. They have each honored their severest critics while yet those critics lived. Their common literature, which tells the story of human liberty in its own tongue, is the richest, most practical and most accessible of all literature, and the popular education upon which rests the freedom of all three is in the same democratic tongue, which is the most widely known of civilized languages and the only unsycophantic speech, for it stands alone in not distinguishing by its use of pronouns in the second person the social grade of the individual addressed.

The future may well realize Rizal's dream that his country should be to Asia what England has been to Europe and the United States is in America, a hope the more likely to be fulfilled since the events of 1898 restored only associations of the earlier and happier days of the history of the Philippines. The very name now used is nearer the spelling of the original Philipinas than the Filipinas of nineteenth century Spanish usage. The first form was used until nearly a century ago, when it was corrupted along with so many things of greater importance.

The Philippines at first were called "The Islands of the West," as they are considered to be occidental and not oriental. They were made known to Europe as a sequel to the discoveries of Columbus. Conquered and colonized from Mexico, most of their pious and charitable endowments, churches, hospitals, asylums and colleges, were endowed by philanthropic Mexicans. Almost as long as Mexico remained Spanish the commerce of the Philippines was confined to Mexico, and the Philippines were a part of the postal system of Mexico and dependent upon the government of Mexico exactly as long as Mexico remained Spanish. They even kept the new world day, one day behind Europe, for a third of a century longer. The Mexican dollars continued to be their chief coins till supplanted, recently, by the present peso, and the highbuttoned white coat, the "americana," by that name was in general use long years ago. The name America is frequently to be found in the old baptismal registers, for a century or more ago many a Filipino child was so christened, and in the '70's Rizal's carving instructor, because so many of the best-made articles he used were of American manufacture, gave the name "Americano" to a godchild. As Americans, Filipinos were joined with the Mexicans when King Ferdinand VII thanked his subjects in both countries for their loyalty during the Napoleonic wars. Filipino students abroad found, too, books about the Philippines listed in libraries and in booksellers' catalogues as a branch of "Americana."

Nor was their acquaintance confined to Spanish Americans. The name "English" was early known. Perhaps no other was more familiar in the beginning, for it was constantly execrated by the Spaniards, and in consequence secretly cherished by those who suffered wrongs at their hands.

Magellan had lost his life in his attempted circumnavigation of the globe and Elcano completed the disastrous voyage in a shattered ship, minus most of its crew. But Drake, an Englishman, undertook the same voyage, passed the Straits in less time than Magellan, and was the first commander in his own ship to put a belt around the earth. These facts were known in the Philippines, and from them the Filipinos drew comparisons unfavorable to the boastful Spaniards.

When the rich Philippine galleon Santa Ana was captured off the California coast by Thomas Candish, "three boys born in Manila" were taken on board the English ships. Afterwards Candish sailed into the straits south of "Luçon" and made friends with the people of the country. There the Filipinos promised "both themselves, and all the islands thereabouts, to aid him whensoever he should come again to overcome the Spaniards."

Dampier, another English sea captain, passed through the Archipelago but little later, and one of his men, John Fitzgerald by name, remained in the Islands, marrying here. He pretended to be a physician, and practiced as a doctor in Manila. There was no doubt room for him, because when Spain expelled the Moors she reduced medicine in her country to a very low state, for the Moors had been her most skilled physicians. Many of these Moors who were Christians, though not orthodox according to the Spanish standard, settled in London, and the English thus profited by the persecution, just as she profited when the cutlery industry was in like manner transplanted from Toledo to Sheffield.

The great Armada against England in Queen Elizabeth's time was an attempt to stop once for all the depredations of her subjects on Spain's commerce in the Orient. As the early Spanish historian, Morga, wrote of it: "Then only the English nation disturbed the Spanish dominion in that Orient. Consequently King Philip desired not only to forbid it with arms near at hand, but also to furnish an example, by their punishment, to all the northern nations, so that they should not undertake the invasions that we see. A beginning was made in this work in the year one thousand five hundred and eighty-eight."

This ingeniously worded statement omits to tell how ignominiously the pretentious expedition ended, but the fact of failure remained and did not help the prestige of Spain, especially among her subjects in the Far East. After all the boastings of what was going to happen, and all the claims of what had been accomplished, the enemies of Spain not only were unchecked but appeared to be bolder than ever. Some of the more thoughtful Filipinos then began to lose confidence in Spanish claims. They were only a few, but their numbers were to increase as the years went by. The Spanish Armada was one of the earliest of those influences which, reënforced by later events, culminated in the life work of José Rizal and the loss of the Philippines by Spain.

At that time the commerce of Manila was restricted to the galleon trade with Mexico, and the prosperity of the Filipino merchants —in large measure the prosperity of the entire Archipelago—depended upon the yearly ventures the hazard of which was not so much the ordinary uncertainty of the sea as the risk of capture by English freebooters. Everybody in the Philippines had heard of these daring English mariners, who were emboldened by an almost unbroken series of successes which had correspondingly discouraged the Spaniards. They carried on unceasing war despite occasional proclamation of peace between England and Spain, for the Spanish treasure ships were tempting prizes, and though at times policy made their government desire friendly relations with Spain, the English people regarded all Spaniards as their natural enemies and all Spanish property as their legitimate spoil.

The Filipinos realized earlier than the Spaniards did that torturing to death shipwrecked English sailors was bad policy. The result was always to make other English sailors fight more desperately to avoid a similar fate. Revenge made them more and more aggressive, and treaties made with Spain were disregarded because, as they said, Spain's inhumanity had forfeited her right to be considered a civilized country.

It was less publicly discussed, but equally well known, that the English freebooters, besides committing countless depredations on commerce, were always ready to lend their assistance to any discontented Spanish subjects whom they could encourage into open rebellion.

The English word Filibuster was changed into "Filibusteros" by the Spanish, and in later years it came to be applied especially to those charged with stirring up discontent and rebellion. For three centuries, in its early application to the losses of commerce, and in its later use as denoting political agitation, possibly no other word in the Philippines, outside of the ordinary expressions of daily life, was so widely known, and certainly none had such sinister signification.

In contrast to this lawless association is a similarity of laws. The followers of Cortez, it will be remembered, were welcomed in Mexico as the long-expected "Fair Gods" because of their blond complexions derived from a Gothic ancestry. Far back in history their forbears had been neighbors of the Anglo-Saxons in the forests of Germany, so that the customs of Anglo-Saxon England and of the Gothic kingdom of Castile had much in common. The "Laws of the Indies," the disregard of which was the ground of most Filipino complaints up to the very last days of the rule of Spain, was a compilation of such of these Anglo-SaxonCastilian laws and customs as it was thought could be extended to the Americas, originally called the New Kingdom of Castile, which included the
Philippine Archipelago. Thus the New England township and the Mexican, and consequently the early Philippine pueblo, as units of local government are nearly related.

These American associations, English influences, and Anglo-Saxon ideals also culminated in the life work of José Rizal, the heir of all the past ages in Philippine history. But other causes operating in his own day— the stories of his elders, the incidents of his childhood, the books he read, the men he met, the travels he made—as later pages will show —contributed further to make him the man he was.

It was fortunate for the Philippines that after the war of misunderstanding with the United States there existed a character that commanded the admiration of both sides. Rizal's writings revealed to the Americans aspirations that appealed to them and conditions that called forth their sympathy, while the Filipinos felt confidence, for that reason, in the otherwise incomprehensible new government which honored their hero.

Rizal was already, and had been for years, without rival as the idol of his countrymen when there came, after deliberation and delay, his official recognition in the Philippines. Necessarily there had to be careful study of his life and scrutiny of his writings before the head of our nation could indorse as the corner stone of the new government which succeeded Spain's misrule, the very ideas which Spain had considered a sufficient warrant for shooting their author as a traitor.

Finally the President of the United States in a public address at Fargo, North Dakota, on April 7, 1903—five years after American scholars had begun to study Philippine affairs as they had never been studied before— declared: "In the Philippine Islands the American government has tried, and is trying, to carry out exactly what the greatest genius and most revered patriot ever known in the Philippines, José Rizal, steadfastly advocated," a formal, emphatic and clear-cut expression of national policy upon a question then of paramount interest.

In the light of the facts of Philippine history already set forth there is no cause for wonder at this sweeping indorsement, even though the views so indorsed were those of a man who lived in conditions widely different from those about to be introduced by the new government. Rizal had not allowed bias to influence him in studying the past history of the Philippines, he had been equally honest with himself in judging the conditions of his own time, and he knew and applied with the same fairness the teaching which holds true in history as in every other branch of science that like causes under like conditions must produce like results, He had been careful in his reasoning, and it stood the test, first of President Roosevelt's advisers, or otherwise that Fargo speech would never have been made, and then of all the President's critics, or there would have been heard more of the statement quoted above which passed unchallenged, but not, one may be sure, uninvestigated.

The American system is in reality not foreign to the Philippines, but it is the highest development, perfected by experience, of the original plan under which the Philippines had prospered and progressed until its benefits were wrongfully withheld from them. Filipino leaders had been vainly asking Spain for the restoration of their rights and the return to the system of the Laws of the Indies. At the time when America came to the Islands there was among them no Rizal, with a knowledge of history that would enable him to recognize that they were getting what they had been wanting, who could rise superior to the unimportant detail of under what name or how the good came as long as it arrived, and whose prestige would have led his countrymen to accept his decision. Some leaders had one qualification, some another, a few combined two, but none had the three, for a country is seldom favored with more than one surpassingly great man at one time.

CHAPTER II

Rizal's Chinese Ancestry

Clustered around the walls of Manila in the latter half of the seventeenth century were little villages the names of which, in some instances slightly changed, are the names of present districts. A fashionable drive then was through the settlement of Filipinos in Bagumbayan—the "new town" to which
Lakandola's subjects had migrated when
Legaspi dispossessed them of their own "Maynila." With the building of the moat this village disappeared, but the name remained, and it is often used to denote the older Luneta, as well as the drive leading to it.

Within the walls lived the Spanish rulers and the few other persons that the fear and jealousy of the Spaniard allowed to come in. Some were Filipinos who ministered to the needs of the Spaniards, but the greater number were Sangleyes, or Chinese, "the mechanics in all trades and excellent workmen," as an old Spanish chronicle says, continuing: "It is true that the city could not be maintained or preserved without the Sangleyes."

The Chinese conditions of these early days are worth recalling, for influences strikingly similar to those which affected the life of José Rizal in his native land were then at work. There were troubled times in the ancient "Middle Kingdom," the earlier name of the corruption of the Malay Tchina (China) by which we know it. The conquering Manchus had placed their emperor on the throne so long occupied by the native dynasty whose adherents had boastingly called themselves "The Sons of Light." The former liberal and progressive government, under which the people prospered, had grown corrupt and helpless, and the country had yielded to the invaders and passed under the terrible tyranny of the Tartars.

Yet there were true patriots among the Chinese who were neither discouraged by these conditions nor blind to the real cause of their misfortunes. They realized that the easy conquest of their country and the utter disregard by their people of the bad government which had preceded it, showed that something was wrong with themselves.

Too wise to exhaust their land by carrying on a hopeless war, they sought rather to get a better government by deserving it, and worked for the general enlightenment, believing that it would offer the most effective opposition to oppression, for they knew well that an intelligent people could not be kept enslaved. Furthermore, they understood that, even if they were freed from foreign rule, the change would be merely to another tyranny unless the darkness of the whole people were dispelled. The few educated men among them would inevitably tyrannize over the ignorant many sooner or later, and it would be less easy to escape from the evils of such misrule, for the opposition to it would be divided, while the strength of union would oppose any foreign despotism. These true patriots were more concerned about the welfare of their country than ambitious for themselves, and they worked to prepare their countrymen for self-government by teaching self-control and respect for the rights of others.

No public effort toward popular education can be made under a bad government. Those opposed to Manchu rule knew of a secret society that had long existed in spite of the laws against it, and they used it as their model in organizing a new society to carry out their purposes. Some of them were members of this Ke-Ming-Tong or Chinese Freemasonry as it is called, and it was difficult for outsiders to find out the differences between it and the new Heaven-Earth-Man Brotherhood. The three parts to their name led the new brotherhood later to be called the Triad Society, and they used a triangle for their seal.

The initiates of the Triad were pledged to one another in a blood compact to "depose the Tsing [Tartar] and restore the Ming [native Chinese] dynasty." But really the society wanted only gradual reform and was against any violent changes. It was at first evolutionary, but later a section became dissatisfied and started another society. The original brotherhood, however, kept on trying to educate its members. It wanted them to realize that the dignity of manhood is above that of rank or riches, and seeking to break down the barriers of different languages and local prejudice, hoped to create an united China efficient in its home government and respected in its foreign relations.

*****

It was the policy of Spain to rule by keeping the different elements among her subjects embittered against one another. Consequently the entire Chinese population of the Philippines had several times been almost wiped out by the Spaniards assisted by the Filipinos and resident Japanese. Although overcrowding was mainly the cause of the Chinese immigration, the considerations already described seem to have influenced the better class of emigrants who incorporated themselves with the Filipinos from 1642 on through the eighteenth century. Apparently these emigrants left their Chinese homes to avoid the shaven crown and long braided queue that the Manchu conquerors were imposing as a sign of submission—a practice recalled by the recent wholesale cutting off of queues which marked the fall of this same Manchu dynasty upon the establishment of the present republic. The patriot Chinese in Manila retained the ancient style, which somewhat resembled the way Koreans arrange their hair. Those who became Christians cut the hair short and wore
European hats, otherwise using the clothing

—blue cotton for the poor, silk for the richer —and felt-soled shoes, still considered characteristically Chinese.
The reasons for the brutal treatment of the unhappy exiles and the causes of the frequent accusation against them that they were intending rebellion may be found in the fear that had been inspired by the Chinese pirates, and the apprehension that the Chinese traders and workmen would take away from the

Filipinos their means of gaining a livelihood. At times unjust suspicions drove some of the less patient to take up arms in self-defense. Then many entirely innocent persons would be massacred, while those who had not bought protection from some powerful Spaniard would have their property pillaged by mobs that protested excessive devotion to Spain and found their patriotism so profitable that they were always eager to stir up trouble.

One of the last native Chinese emperors, not wishing that any of his subjects should live outside his dominions, informed the Spanish authorities that he considered the emigrants evil persons unworthy of his interest. His Manchu successors had still more reason to be careless of the fate of the Manila Chinese. They were consequently ill treated with impunity, while the Japanese were "treated very cordially, as they are a race that demand good treatment, and it is advisable to do so for the friendly relations between the Islands and Japan," to quote the ancient history once more.

Pagan or Christian, a Chinaman's life in Manila then was not an enviable one, though the Christians were slightly more secure. The Chinese quarter was at first inside the city, but before long it became a considerable district of several streets along Arroceros near the present Botanical Garden. Thus the Chinese were under the guns of the Bastion San Gabriel, which also commanded two other Chinese settlements across the river in Tondo—Minondoc, or Binondo, and Baybay. They had their own headmen, their own magistrates and their own prison, and no outsiders were permitted among them. The Dominican Friars, who also had a number of missionary stations in China, maintained a church and a hospital for these Manila Chinese and established a settlement where those who became Christians might live with their families. Writers of that day suggest that sometimes conversions were prompted by the desire to get married—which until 1898 could not be done outside the Church—or to help the convert's business or to secure the protection of an influential Spanish godfather, rather than by any changed belief.

Certainly two of these reasons did not influence the conversion of Doctor Rizal's paternal ancestor, Lam-co (that is, "Lam, Esq."), for this Chinese had a Chinese godfather and was not married till many years later.

He was a native of the Chinchew district, where the Jesuits first, and later the
Dominicans, had had missions, and he perhaps knew something of Christianity before leaving China. One of his church records indicates his home more definitely, for it specifies Siongque, near the great city, an agricultural community, and in China cultivation of the soil is considered the most honorable employment. Curiously enough, without conversion, the people of that region even to-day consider themselves akin to the Christians. They believe in one god and have characteristics distinguishing them from the Pagan Chinese, possibly derived from some remote Mohammedan ancestors.

Lam-co's prestige among his own people, as shown by his leadership of those who later settled with him in Biñan, as well as the fact that even after his residence in the country he was called to Manila to act as godfather, suggests that he was above the ordinary standing, and certainly not of the coolie class. This is bogne out by his marrying the daughter of an educated Chinese, an alliance that was not likely to have been made unless he was a person of some education, and education is the Chinese test of social degree.

He was baptized in the Parian church of San Gabriel on a Sunday in June of 1697. Lamco's age was given in the record as thirty-five years, and the names of his parents were given as Siang-co and Zun-nio. The second syllables of these names are titles of a little more respect than the ordinary "Mr." and "Mrs.," something like the Spanish Don and Doña, but possibly the Dominican priest who kept the register was not so careful in his use of Chinese words as a Chinese would have been. Following the custom of the other converts on the same occasion, Lam-co took the name Domingo, the Spanish for Sunday, in honor of the day. The record of this baptism is still to be seen in the records of the Parian church of San Gabriel, which are preserved with the Binondo records, in Manila.

Chinchew, the capital of the district from which he came, was a literary center and a town famed in Chinese history for its loyalty; it was probably the great port Zeitung which so strongly impressed the Venetian traveler Marco Polo, the first European to see China.

The city was said by later writers to be large and beautiful and to contain half a million inhabitants, "candid, open and friendly people, especially friendly and polite to foreigners." It was situated forty miles from the sea, in the province of Fokien, the rocky coast of which has been described as resembling Scotland, and its sturdy inhabitants seem to have borne some resemblance to the Scotch in their love of liberty. The district now is better known by its present port of Amoy.

Altogether, in wealth, culture and comfort, Lam-co's home city far surpassed the Manila of that day, which was, however, patterned after it. The walls of Manila, its paved streets, stone bridges, and large houses with spacious courts are admitted by Spanish writers to be due to the industry and skill of Chinese workmen. They were but slightly changed from their Chinese models, differing mainly in ornamentation, so that to a Chinese the city by the Pasig, to which he gave the name of "the city of horses," did not seem strange, but reminded him rather of his own country.

Famine in his native district, or the plague which followed it, may have been the cause of Lam-co's leaving home, but it was more probably political troubles which transferred to the Philippines that intelligent and industrious stock whose descendants have proved such loyal and creditable sons of their adopted country. Chinese had come to the Islands centuries before the Spaniards arrived and they are still coming, but no other period has brought such a remarkable contribution to the strong race which the mixture of many peoples has built up in the Philippines. Few are the Filipinos notable in recent history who cannot trace descent from a Chinese baptized in San Gabriel church during the century following 1642; until recently many have felt ashamed of these really creditable ancestors.

Soon after Lam-co came to Manila he made the acquaintance of two wellknown Dominicans and thus made friendships that changed his career and materially affected the fortunes of his descendants. These powerful friends were the learned Friar Francisco Marquez, author of a Chinese grammar, and
Friar Juan Caballero, a former missionary in China, who, because of his own work and because his brother held high office there, was influential in the business affairs of the Order. Through them Lam-co settled in Biñan, on the Dominican estate named after "St. Isidore the Laborer." There, near where the Pasig river flows out of the Laguna de Bay, Lamco's descendants were to be tenants until another government, not yet born, and a system unknown in his day, should end a long series of inevitable and vexatious disputes by buying the estate and selling it again, on terms practicable for them, to those who worked the land.

The Filipinos were at law over boundaries and were claiming the property that had been early and cheaply acquired by the Order as endowment for its university and other charities. The Friars of the Parian quarter thought to take those of their parishioners in whom they had most confidence out of harm's way, and by the same act secure more satisfactory tenants, for prejudice was then threatening another indiscriminate massacre. So they settled many industrious Chinese converts upon these farms, and flattered themselves that their tenant troubles were ended, for these foreigners could have no possible claim to the land. The Chinese were equally pleased to have safer homes and an occupation which in China placed them in a social position superior to that of a tradesman.

Domingo Lam-co was influential in building up Tubigan barrio, one of the richest parts of the great estate. In name and appearance it recalled the fertile plains that surrounded his native Chinchew, "the city of springs." His neighbors were mainly Chinchew men, and what is of more importance to this narrative, the wife whom he married just before removing to the farm was of a good Chinchew family. She was Inez de la Rosa and but half Domingo's age; they were married in the Parian church by the same priest who over thirty years before had baptized her husband.

Her father was Agustin Chinco, also of Chinchew, a rice merchant, who had been baptized five years earlier than Lam-co. His baptismal record suggests that he was an educated man, as already indicated, for the name of his town proved a puzzle till a present-day Dominican missionary from Amoy explained that it appeared to be the combined names for Chinchew in both the common and literary Chinese, in each case with the syllable denoting the town left off.
Apparently when questioned from what town he came, Chinco was careful not to repeat the word town, but gave its name only in the literary language, and when that was not understood, he would repeat it in the local dialect. The priest, not understanding the significance of either in that form, wrote down the two together as a single word. Knowledge of the literary Chinese, or Mandarin, as it is generally called, marked the educated man, and, as we have already pointed out, education in China meant social position. To such minute deductions is it necessary to resort when records are scarce, and to be of value the explanation must be in harmony with the conditions of the period; subsequent research has verified the foregoing conclusions.

Agustin Chinco had also a Chinese godfather and his parents were Chinco and Zun-nio.

He was married to Jacinta Rafaela, a Chinese mestiza of the Parian, as soon after his baptism as the banns could be published. She apparently was the daughter of a Christian Chinese and a Chinese mestiza; there were too many of the name Jacinta in that day to identify which of the several Jacintas she was and so enable us to determine the names of her parents. The Rafaela part of her name was probably added after she was grown up, in honor of the patron of the Parian settlement, San Rafael, just as Domingo, at his marriage, added Antonio in honor of the Chinese. How difficult guides names then were may be seen from this list of the six children of Agustin Chinco and Jacinta Rafaela: Magdalena

Vergara, Josepha, Cristoval de la Trinidad, Juan Batista, Francisco HongSun and Inez de la Rosa.

The father-in-law and the son-in-law, Agustin and Domingo, seem to have been old friends, and apparently of the same class. Lam-co must have seen his future wife, the youngest in Chinco's numerous family, grow up from babyhood, and probably was attracted by the idea that she would make a good housekeeper like her thrifty mother, rather than by any romantic feelings, for sentiment entered very little into matrimony in those days when the parents made the matches. Possibly, however, their married life was just as happy, for divorces then were not even thought of, and as this couple prospered they apparently worked well together in a financial way.

The next recorded event in the life of
Domingo Lam-co and his wife occurred in 1741 when, after years of apparently happy existence in Biñan, came a great grief in the loss of their baby daughter, Josepha Didnio, probably named for her aunt. She had lived only five days, but payments to the priest for a funeral such as was not given to many grown persons who died that year in Biñan show how keenly the parents felt the loss of their little girl. They had at the time but one other child, a boy of ten, Francisco Mercado, whose Christian name was given partly because he had an uncle of the same name, and partly as a tribute of gratitude to the friendly Friar scholar in Manila. His new surname suggests that the family possessed the commendable trait of taking pride in its ancestry.

Among the Chinese the significance of a name counts for much and it is always safe to seek a reason for the choice of a name. The Lam-co family

were not given to the practice of taking the names of their god-parents. Mercado recalls both an honest Spanish encomendero of the region, also named Francisco, and a worthy mestizo Friar, now remembered for his botanical studies, but it is not likely that these influenced Domingo Lamco in choosing this name for his son. He gave his boy a name which in the careless Castilian of the country was but a Spanish translation of the Chinese name by which his ancestors had been called. Sangley, Mercado and Merchant mean much the same;
Francisco therefore set out in life with a surname that would free him from the prejudice that followed those with Chinese names, and yet would remind him of his Chinese ancestry. This was wisdom, for seldom are men who are ashamed of their ancestry any credit to it.

The family history has to be gleaned from partially preserved parochial registers of births, marriages and deaths, incomplete court records, the scanty papers of the estates, a few land transfers, and some stray writings that accidentally have been preserved with the latter. The next event in Domingo's life which is revealed by them is a visit to Manila where in the old Parian church he acted as sponsor, or godfather, at the baptism of a countryman, and a new convert, Siong-co, whose granddaughter was, we shall see, to marry a grandson of Lam-co's, the couple becoming Rizal's grandparents.

Francisco was a grown man when his mother died and was buried with the elaborate ceremonies which her husband's wealth permitted. There was a coffin, a niche in which to put it, chanting of the service and special prayers. All these involved extra cost, and the items noted in the margin of her funeral record make a total which in those days was a considerable sum. Domingo outlived Mrs. Lam-co by but a few years, and he also had, for the time, an expensive funeral.

CHAPTER III

Liberalizing Hereditary Influences

The hope of the Biñan landlords that by changing from Filipino to Chinese tenantry they could avoid further litigation seems to have been disappointed. A family tradition of Francisco Mercado tells of a tedious and costly lawsuit with the Order. Its details and merits are no longer remembered, and they are not important.

History has recorded enough agrarian trouble, in all ages and in all countries, to prove the economic mistake of large holdings of land

by those who do not cultivate it. Human nature is alike the world over, it does not change with the centuries, and just as the Filipinos had done, the Chinese at last obiected to paying increased rent for improvements which they made themselves.

A Spanish iudge required the landlords to produce their deeds, and, after measuring the land, he decided that they were then taking rent for considerably more than they had originally bought or had been given. But the tenants lost on the appeal, and, as they thought it was because they were weak and their opponents powerful, a grievance grew up which was still remembered in Rizal's day and was well known and understood by him.

Another cause of discontent, which was a liberalizing influence, was making itself felt in the Philippines about the time of Domingo's death. A number of Spaniards had been claiming for their own countrymen such safeguards of personal liberty as were enjoyed by Englishmen, for no other government in Europe then paid any attention to the rights of the individual. Learned men had devoted much study to the laws and rights of nations, but these Spanish Liberals insisted that it was the guarantees given to the citizens, and not the political independence of the State, that made a country really free. Unfortunately, just as their proposals began to gain followers, Spain became involved in war with England, because the Spanish King, then as now a Bourbon and so related to a number of other reactionary rulers, had united in the family compact by which the royal relatives were to stamp out liberal ideas in their own dominions, and as allies to crush England, the source of the dissatisfaction which threatened their thrones.

Many progressive Spaniards had become Freemasons, when that ancient society, after its revival in England, had been reintroduced into Spain. Now they found themselves suspected of sympathy with England and therefore of treason to Spain. While this could not be proved, it led to enforcing a papal bull against them, by which Pope Clement XII placed their institution under the ban of excommunication.

At first it was intended to execute all the Spanish Freemasons, but the Queen's favorite violinist secretly sympathized with them. He used his influence with Her Majesty so well that through her intercession the King commuted the sentences from death to banishment as minor officials in the possessions overseas.

Thus Cuba, Mexico, South and Central America, and the Philippines were provided with the ablest Spanish advocates of modern ideas. In no other way could liberalism have been spread so widely or more effectively.

Besides these officeholders there had been from the earliest days noblemen, temporarily out of favor at Court, in banishment in the colonies. Cavite had some of these exiles, who were called "caja abierta," or carte blanche, because their generous allowances, which could be drawn whenever there were government funds, seemed without limit to the Filipinos. The Spanish residents of the Philippines were naturally glad to entertain, supply money to, and otherwise serve these men of noble birth, who might at any time be restored to favor and again be influential, and this gave them additional prestige in the eyes of the Filipinos. One of these exiles, whose descendants yet live in these Islands, passed from prisoner in Cavite to viceroy in Mexico.

Francisco Mercado lived near enough to hear of the "cajas abiertas" (exiles) and their ways, if he did not actually meet some of them and personally experience the charm of their courtesy. They were as different from the ruder class of Spaniards who then were coming to the

Islands as the few banished officials were unlike the general run of officeholders. The contrast naturally suggested that the majority of the Spaniards in the Philippines, both in official and in private life, were not creditable representatives of their country. This charge, insisted on with greater vehemence as subsequent events furnished further reasons for doing so, embittered the controversies of the last century of Spanish rule. The very persons who realized that the accusation was true of themselves, were those who most resented it, and the opinion of them which they knew the Filipinos held but dared not voice, rankled in their breasts. They welcomed every disparagement of the Philippines and its people, and thus made profitable a senseless and abusive campaign which was carried on by unscrupulous, irresponsible writers of such defective education that vilification was their sole argument. Their charges were easily disproved, but they had enough cunning to invent new charges continually, and prejudice gave ready credence to them.

Finally an unreasoning fury broke out and in blind passion innocent persons were struck down; the taste for blood once aroused, irresponsible writers like that Retana who has now become Rizal's biographer, whetted the savage appetite for fresh victims. The last fifty years of Spanish rule in the Philippines was a small saturnalia of revenge with hardly a lucid interval for the governing power to reflect or an opportunity for the reasonable element to intervene. Somewhat similarly the Bourbons in France had hoped to postpone the day of reckoning for their mistakes by misdeeds done in fear to terrorize those who sought reforms. The aristocracy of France paid back tenfold each drop of innocent blood that was shed, but while the unreasoning world recalls the French Revolution with horror, the student of history thinks more of the evils which made it a natural result. Mirabeau in vain sought to restrain his aroused countrymen, just as he had vainly pleaded with the aristocrats to end their excesses. Rizal, who held Mirabeau for his hero among the men of the French Revolution, knew the historical lesson and sought to sound a warning, but he was unheeded by the Spaniards and misunderstood by many of his countrymen.

At about the time of the arrival of the Spanish political exiles we find in Manila a proof of the normal mildness of Spain in the Philippines. The Inquisition, of dread name elsewhere, in the Philippines affected only Europeans, had before it two Englishspeaking persons, an Irish doctor and a county merchant accused of being
Freemasons. The kind-hearted Friar inquisitor dismissed the culprits with warnings, and excepting some Spanish political matters in which it took part, this was the nearest that the institution ever came to exercising its functions here.

The sufferings of the Indians in the SpanishAmerican gold mines, too, had no Philippine counterpart, for at the instance of the friars the Church early forbade the enslaving of the people. Neither friars nor government have any records in the Philippines which warrant belief that they were responsible for the severe punishments of the period from '72 to '98. Both were connected with opposition to reforms which appeared likely to jeopardize their property or to threaten their prerogatives, and in this they were only human, but here their selfish interests and activities seem to cease.

For religious reasons the friar orders combatted modern ideas which they feared might include atheistical teachings such as had made trouble in France, and the Government was against the introduction of latter-day thought of democratic tendency, but in both instances the opposition may well have been believed to be for the best interest of the Philippine people. However mistaken, their action can only be deplored not censured. The black side of this matter was the rousing of popular passion, and it was done by sheets subsidized to argue; their editors, however, resorted to abuse in order to conceal the fact that they had not the ability to perform the services for which they were hired. While some individual members of both the religious orders and of the Government were influenced by these inflaming attacks, the interests concerned, as organizations, seem to have had a policy of self-defense, and not of revenge.

The theory here advanced must wait for the judgment of the reader till the later events have been submitted. However, Rizal himself may be called in to prove that the record and policy is what has been asserted, for otherwise he would hardly have disregarded, as he did, the writings of Motley and Prescott, historians whom he could have quoted with great advantage to support the attacks he would surely have not failed to make had they seemed to him warranted, for he never was wanting in knowledge, resourcefulness or courage where his country was concerned.

No definite information is available as to what part Francisco Mercado took during the disturbed two years when the English held Manila and Judge Anda carried on a guerilla warfare. The Dominicans were active in enlisting their tenants to fight against the invaders, and probably he did his share toward the Spanish defense either with contributions or personal service. The attitude of the region in which he lived strengthens this surmise, for only after long-continued wrongs and repeatedly broken promises of redress did Filipino loyalty fail. This was a century too early for the country around Manila, which had been better protected and less abused than the provinces to the north where the Ilokanos revolted.

Biñan, however, was within the sphere of English influence, for Anda's campaign was not quite so formidable as the inscription on his monument in Manila represents it to be, and he was far indeed from being the great conqueror that the tablet on the Santa Cruz Church describes him. Because of its nearness to Manila and Cavite and its rich gardens, British soldiers and sailors often visited Biñan, but as the inhabitants never found occasion to abandon their homes, they evidently suffered no serious inconvenience.

Commerce, a powerful factor, destroying the hermit character of the Islands, gained by the short experience of freer trade under England's rule, since the Filipinos obtained a taste for articles before unused, which led them to be discontented and insistent, till the Manila market finally came to be better supplied. The contrast of the British judicial system with the Spanish tribunals was also a revelation, for the foulest blot upon the colonial administration of Spain was her iniquitous courts of justice, and this was especially true of the Philippines.

Anda's triumphal entry into the capital was celebrated with a wholesale hanging of Chinese, which must have made Francisco Mercado glad that he was now so identified with the country as to escape the prejudice against his race.

A few years later came the expulsion of the Jesuit fathers and the confiscation of their property. It certainly weakened the government; personal acquaintance counted largely with the Filipinos; whole parishes knew Spain and the Church only through their parish priest, and the parish priest was usually a Jesuit whose courtesy equalled that of the most aristocratic officeholder or of any exiled "caja abierta."

Francisco Mercado did not live in a Jesuit parish but in the neighboring hacienda of St. John the Baptist at Kalamba, where there was a great dam and an extensive irrigation system which caused the land to rival in fertility the rich soil of Biñan. Everybody in his neighborhood knew that the estate had been purchased with money left in Mexico by pious Spaniards who wanted to see Christianity spread in the Philippines, and it seemed to them sacrilege that the government should take such property for its own secular uses.

The priests in Biñan were Filipinos and were usually leaders among the secular clergy, for the parish was desirable beyond most in the archdiocese because of its nearness to Manila, its excellent climate, its well-to-do parishioners and the great variety of its useful and ornamental plants and trees. Many of the fruits and vegetables of Biñan were little known elsewhere, for they were of American origin, brought by Dominicans on the voyages from Spain by way of Mexico. They were introduced first into the great gardens at the hacienda house, which was a comfortable and spacious building adjoining the church, and the favorite resting place for members of the Order in Manila.

The attendance of the friars on Sundays and fête days gave to the religious services on these occasions a dignity usually belonging to city churches. Sometimes, too, some of the missionaries from China and other Dominican notables would be seen in Biñan. So the people not only had more of the luxuries and the pomp of life than most Filipinos, but they had a broader outlook upon it. Their opinion of Spain was formed from acquaintance with many Spaniards and from comparing them with people of other lands who often came to Manila and investigated the region close to it, especially the show spots such as Biñan. Then they were on the road to the fashionable baths at Los Baños, where the higher officials often resorted. Such opportunities gave a sort of education, and Biñan people were in this way more cultured than the dwellers in remote places, whose only knowledge of their sovereign state was derived from a single Spaniard, the friar curate of their parish.

Monastic training consists in withdrawing from the world and living isolated under strict rule, and this would scarcely seem to be the best preparation for such responsibility as was placed upon the Friars. Troubles were bound to come, and the people of Biñan, knowing the ways of the world, would soon be likely to complain and demand the changes which would avoid them; the residents of less worldly wise communities would wait and suffer till too late, and then in blind wrath would wreak bloody vengeance upon guilty and innocent alike.

Kalamba, a near neighbor of Biñan, had other reasons for being known besides its confiscation by the government. It was the scene of an early and especially cruel massacre of Chinese, and about Francisco's time considerable talk had been occasioned because an archbishop had established an uniform scale of charges for the various rites of the Church. While these charges were often complained of, it was the poorer people (some of whom were in receipt of charity) who suffered. The rich were seeking more expensive ceremonies in order to outshine the other well-to-do people of their neighborhood. The real grievance was, however, not the cost, but the fact that political discriminations were made so that those who were out of favor with the government were likewise deprived of church privileges. The reform of Archbishop Santo y Rufino has importance only because it gave the people of the provinces what Manila had long possessed—a knowledge of the rivalry between the secular and the regular clergy.

The people had learned in Governor Bustamente's time that Church and State did not always agree, and now they saw dissensions within the Church. The Spanish Conquest and the possession of the Philippines had been made easy by the doctrine of the indivisibility of Church and State, by the teaching that the two were one and inseparable, but events were continually demonstrating the falsity of this early teaching. Hence the foundation of the sovereignty of Spain was slowly weakening, and nowhere more surely than in the region near Manila which numbered José Rizal's keen-witted and observing great grandfather among its leading men.

Francisco Mercado was a bachelor during the times of these exciting events and therefore more free to visit Manila and Cavite, and he was possibly the more likely to be interested in political matters. He married on May 26, 1771, rather later in life than was customary in Biñan, though he was by no means as old as his father, Domingo, was when he married. His bride, Bernarda Monicha, was a Chinese mestiza of the neighboring hacienda of San Pedro Tunasan, who had been early orphaned and from childhood had lived in Biñan. As the coadjutor priest of the parish bore the same name, one uncommon in the Biñan
records of that period, it is possible that he was a relative. The frequent occurrence of the name of Monicha among the last names of girls of that vicinity later on must be ascribed to Bernarda's popularity as godmother.

Mr. and Mrs. Francisco Mercado had two children, both boys, Juan and Clemente. During their youth the people of the Philippines were greatly interested in the struggles going on between England, the old enemy of Spain, and the rebellious EnglishAmerican colonies. So bitter was the Spanish hatred of the nation which had humiliated her repeatedly on both land and sea, that the authorities forgot their customary caution

and encouraged the circulation of any story that told in favor of the American colonies. Little did they realize the impression that the statement of grievances—so trivial compared
with the injustices that were being inflicted upon the Spanish colonials—was making upon their subjects overseas, who until then had been carefully guarded from all modern ideas of government. American successes were hailed with enthusiasm in the most remote towns, and from this time may be dated a perceptible increase in Philippine discontent. Till then outbreaks and uprisings had been more for revenge than with any well-considered aim, but henceforth complaints became definite, demands were made that to an increasing number of people appeared to be reasonable, and those demands were denied or ignored, or promises were made in answer to them which were never fulfilled.

Francisco Mercado was well to do, if we may judge from the number of carabaos he presented for registration, for his was among the largest herds in the book of brands that has chanced to be preserved with the Biñan church records. In 1783 he was alcalde, or chief officer of the town, and he lived till 1801. His name appears so often as godfather in the registers of baptisms and weddings that he must have been a goodnatured, liberal and popular man.

Mrs. Francisco Mercado survived her husband by a number of years, and helped to nurse through his baby ailments a grandson also named Francisco, the father of Doctor Rizal.

Francisco Mercado's eldest son, Juan, built a fine house in the center of Biñan, where its pretentious stone foundations yet stand to attest how the home deserved the pride which the family took in it.

At twenty-two Juan married a girl of
Tubigan, who was two years his elder, Cirila
Alejandra, daughter of Domingo Lam-co's Chinese godson, Siong-co. Cirila's father's silken garments were preserved by the family until

within the memory of persons now living, and it is likely that José Rizal, Siongco's great-grandson, while in school at Biñan, saw these tangible proofs of the social standing in China of this one of his ancestors.

Juan Mercado was three times the chief officer of Biñan—in 1808, 1813 and 1823. His sympathies are evident from the fact that he gave the second name, Fernando, to the son born when the French were trying to get the Filipinos to declare for King Joseph, whom his brother Napoleon had named sovereign of Spain. During the little while that the Philippines profited by the first constitution of Spain, Mercado was one of the two alcaldes. King Ferdinand VII then was relying on English aid, and to please his allies as well as to secure the loyalty of his subjects, Ferdinand pretended to be a very liberal monarch, swearing to uphold the constitution which the representatives of the people had framed at Cadiz in 1812. Under this constitution the Filipinos were to be represented in the Spanish Cortes, and the grandfather of Rizal was one of the electors to choose the Representative.

During the next twenty-five years the history of the connection of the Philippines with Spain is mainly a record of the breaking and renewing of the King's oaths to the constitution, and of the Philippines electing delegates who would find the Cortes dissolved by the time they could get to Madrid, until in the final constitution that did last Philippine representation was left out altogether. Had things been different the sad story of this book might never have been told, for though the misgovernment of the Philippines was originally owing to the disregard for the Laws of the Indies and to giving unrestrained power to officials, the effects of these mistakes were not apparent until well into the nineteenth century.

Another influence which educated the Filipino people was at work during this period. They had heard the American Revolution extolled and its course approved, because the Spaniards disliked England. Then came the French Revolution, which appalled the civilized world. A people, ignorant and oppressed, washed out in blood the wrongs which they had suffered, but their liberty degenerated into license, their ideals proved impracticable, and the anarchy of their radical republic was succeeded by the military despotism of Napoleon.

A book written in Tagalog by a friar pointed out the differences between true liberty and false. It was the story of an old municipal captain who had traveled and returned to enlighten his friends at home. The story was well told, and the catechism form in which, by his friends' questions and the answers to them, the author's opinions were presented, was familiar to Filipinos, so that there were many intelligent readers, but its results were quite different from what its pious and patriotic author had intended they should be.

The book told of the broadening influences of travel and of education; it suggested that liberty was possible only for the intelligent, but that schools, newspapers, libraries and the means of travel which the American colonists were enjoying were not provided for the Filipinos.

They were further told that the Spanish colonies in America were repeating the unhappy experiences of the French republic, while the "English North Americans," whose ships during the American Revolution had found the Pacific a safe refuge from England, had developed considerable commerce with the Philippines. A kindly feeling toward the Americans had been aroused by the praise given to Filipino mechanics who had been trained by an American naval officer to repair his ship when the Spaniards at the government dockyards proved incapable of doing the work. Even the first American Consul, whose monument yet remains in the Plaza Cervantes, Manila, though, because of his faith, he could not be buried in the consecrated ground of the Catholic cemeteries, received what would appear to be a higher honor, a grave in the principal business plaza of the city.

The inferences were irresistible: the way of the French Revolution was repugnant alike to God and government, that of the American was approved by both. Filipinos of reflective turn of mind began to study America; some even had gone there; for, from a little Filipino settlement,

St. Malo near New Orleans, sailors enlisted to fight in the second war of the United States against England; one of them was wounded and his name was long borne on the pension roll of the United States.

The danger of the dense ignorance in which their rulers kept the Filipinos showed itself in 1819, when a French ship from India having introduced Asiatic cholera into the Islands, the lowest classes of Manila ascribed it to the collections of insects and reptiles which a French naturalist, who was a passenger upon the ship, had brought ashore. However the story started, the collection and the dwelling of the naturalist fared badly, and afterwards the mob, excited by its success, made war upon all foreigners. At length the excitement subsided, but too much damage to foreign lives and property had been done to be ignored, and the matter had an ugly look, especially as no Spaniard had suffered by this outbreak. The Insular government roused itself to punish some of the minor misdoers and made many explanations and apologies, but the aggrieved nations insisted, and obtained as compensation a greater security for foreigners and the removal of many of the restraints upon commerce and travel. Thus the riot proved a substantial step in Philippine progress.

Following closely the excitement over the massacre of the foreigners in Manila came the news that Spain had sold Florida to the United States. The circumstances of the sale were hardly creditable to the vendor, for it was under compulsion. Her lax government had permitted its territory to become the refuge of criminals and lawless savages who terrorized the border until in self-defense American soldiers under General Jackson had to do the work that Spain could not do. Then with order restored and the country held by American troops, an offer to purchase was made to Spain who found the liberal purchase money a very welcome addition to her bankrupt treasury.

Immediately after this the Monroe Doctrine attracted widespread attention in the Philippines. Its story is part of Spanish history. A group of reactionary sovereigns of Europe, including King Ferdinand, had united to crush out progressive ideas in their kingdoms and to remove the dangerous examples of liberal states from their neighborhoods. One of the effects of this unholy alliance was to nullify all the reforms which Spain had introduced to secure English assistance in her time of need, and the people of England were greatly incensed. Great Britain had borne the brunt of the war against Napoleon because her liberties were jeopardized, but naturally her people could not be expected to undertake further warfare merely for the sake of people of another land, however they might sympathize with them.

George Canning, the English statesman to whom belonged much of the credit for the Constitution of Cadiz, thought out a way to punish the Spanish king for his perfidy. King Ferdinand was planning, with the Island of Cuba as a base, to begin a campaign that should return his rebellious American colonies to their allegiance, for they had taken advantage of disturbances in the Peninsula to declare their independence. England proposed to the United States that they, the two Anglo-Saxon nations whose ideas of liberty had unsettled Europe and whom the alliance would have attacked had it dared, should unite in a protectorate over the New World. England was to guard the sea and the United States were to furnish the soldiers for any land fighting which might come on their side of the Atlantic.

World politics had led the enemies of England to help her revolting colonies, Napoleon's jealousy of Britain had endowed the new nation with the vast Louisiana Territory, and European complications saved the United States from the natural consequences of their disastrous war of 1812, which taught them that union was as necessary to preserve their independence as it had been to win it. Canning's project in principle appealed to the North Americans, but the study of it soon showed that Great Britain was selfish in her suggestion. After a generation of fighting, England found herself drained of soldiers and therefore she diplomatically invited the coöperation of her former colonies; but, regardless of any formal arrangement, her navy could be relied on to prevent those who had played her false from transporting large armies across the ocean into the neighborhood of her otherwise defenseless colonies. That was selfpreservation.

President Monroe's advisers were willing that their country should run some risk on its own account, but they had the traditional American aversion to entangling alliances. So the Cabinet counseled that the young nation alone should make itself the protector of the South American republics, and drafted the declaration warning the world that aggression against any of the New World democracies would be resented as unfriendliness to the United States.

It was the firm attitude of President Monroe that compelled Spain to forego the attempt to reconquer her former colonies, and therefore Mexico and Central and South America owe their existence as republics quite as much to the elder commonwealth as does Cuba.

The American attitude revealed in the Monroe Doctrine was especially obnoxious to the Spaniards in the Philippines but their intemperate denunciations of the policy of America for the Americans served only to spread a knowledge of that doctrine among the people of that little territory which remained to them to misgovern. Secretly there began to be, among the stouter-hearted Filipinos, some who cherished a corollary to the Monroe Doctrine, the Philippines for the Filipinos.

Thoughts of separation from Spain by means of rebellion, by sale and by the assistance of other nations, had been thus put into the heads of the people. These were all changes coming from outside, but it next to be demonstrated that Spain herself did not hold her noncontiguous territories as sacred as she did her home dominions.

The sale of Florida suggested that Cuba, Porto Rico and the Philippines were also available assets, and an offer to sell them was made to the King of France; but this sovereign overreached himself, for, thinking to drive a better bargain, he claimed that the low prices were too high. Thereupon the Spanish Ambassador, who was not in accord with his unpatriotic instructions, at once withdrew the offer and the negotiations terminated.

But the Spanish people learned of the proposed sale and their indignation was great. The news spread to the Spaniards in the Philippines. Through their comments the Filipinos realized that the much-talked-of sacred integrity of the Spanish dominions was a meaningless phrase, and that the Philippines would not always be Spanish if Spain could get her price.

Gobernadorcillo Mercado, "Captain Juan," as he was called, made a creditable figure in his office, and there used to be in Biñan a painting of him with his official sword, cocked hat and embroidered blouse. The municipal executive in his time did not always wear the ridiculous combination of European and old Tagalog costumes, namely, a high hat and a short jacket over the floating tails of a pleated shirt, which later undignified the position. He has a notable record for his generosity, the absence of oppression and for the official honesty which distinguished his public service from that of many who held his same office. He did, however, change the tribute lists so that his family were no longer "Chinese mestizos," but were enrolled as "Indians," the wholesale Spanish term for the natives of all Spain's possessions overseas. This, in a way, was compensation (it lowered his family's tribute) for his having to pay the taxes of all who died in Biñan or moved away during his term of office. The municipal captain then was held accountable whether the people could pay or not, no deductions ever being made from the lists. Most gobernadorcillos found ways to reimburse themselves, but not Mercado. His family, however, were of the fourth generation in the Philippines and he evidently thought that they were entitled to be called Filipinos.

A leader in church work also, and several times "Hermano mayor" of its charitable society, the Captain's name appears on a number of lists that have come down from that time as a liberal contributor to various public subscriptions. His wife was equally benevolent, as the records show.

Mr. and Mrs. Mercado did not neglect their family, which was rather numerous. Their children were Gavino, Potenciana (who never married),

Leoncio, Fausto, Barcelisa (who became the wife of Hermenegildo Austria),
Gabriel, Julian, Gregorio Fernando, Casimiro,
Petrona (who married Gregorio Neri),

Tomasa (later Mrs. F. de Guzman), and Cornelia, the belle of the family, who later lived in Batangas.

Young Francisco was only eight years old when his father died, but his mother and sister Potenciana looked well after him. First he attended a Biñan Latin school, and later he seems to have studied Latin and philosophy in the College of San José in Manila.

A sister, Petrona, for some years had been a dressgoods merchant in nearby Kalamba, on an estate that had recently come under the same ownership as Biñan. There she later married, and shortly after was widowed. Possibly upon their mother's death,
Potenciana and Francisco removed to Kalamba; though Petrona died not long after, her brother and sister continued to make their home there.

Francisco, in spite of his youth, became a tenant of the estate as did some others of his family, for their Biñan holdings were not large enough to give farms to all Captain Juan's many sons. The landlords early recognized the agricultural skill of the Mercados by further allotments, as they could bring more land under cultivation. Sometimes Francisco was able to buy the holdings of others who proved less successful in their management and became discouraged.

The pioneer farming, clearing the miasmatic forests especially, was dangerous work, and there were few families that did not buy their land with the lives of some of its members. In 1847 the Mercados had funerals, of brothers and nephews of Francisco, and, chief among them, of that elder sister who had devoted her life to him, Potenciana. She had always prompted and inspired the young man, and Francisco's success in life was largely due to her wise counsels and her devoted encouragement of his industry and ambition. Her thrifty management of the home, too, was sadly missed.

A year after his sister Potenciana's death,
Francisco Mercado married Teodora Alonzo, a native of Manila, who for several years had been residing with her mother at Kalamba. The history of the family of Mrs. Mercado is unfortunately not so easily traced as is that of her husband, and what is known is of less simplicity and perhaps of more interest since the mother's influence is greater than the father's, and she was the mother of José Rizal.

Her father, Lorenzo Alberto Alonzo (born
1790, died 1854), is said to have been "very Chinese" in appearance. He had a brother who was a priest, and a sister, Isabel, who was quite wealthy; he himself was also well to do. Their mother, Maria Florentina (born 1771, died 1817), was, on her mother's side, of the famous Florentina family of Chinese mestizos originating in Baliwag, Bulacan, and her father was Captain Mariano Alejandro of Biñan.

Lorenzo Alberto was municipal captain of
Biñan in 1824, as had been his father, Captain Cipriano Alonzo (died 1805), in 1797. The grandfather, Captain Gregorio Alonzo (died 1794), was a native of Quiotan barrio, and twice, in 1763 and again in 1768, at the head of the mestizos' organization of the Santa Cruz district in Manila.

Captain Lorenzo was educated for a surveyor, and his engineering books, some in English and others in French, were preserved in Biñan till, upon the death of his son, the family belongings were scattered. He was wealthy, and had invested a considerable sum of money with the American Manila shipping firms of Peele, Hubbell & Co., and Russell, Sturgis & Co.

The family story is that he became acquainted with Brigida de Quintos, Mrs. Rizal's mother, while he was a student in Manila, and that she, being unusually well educated for a girl of those days, helped him with his mathematics. Their acquaintance apparently arose through relationship, both being connected with the Reyes family. They had five children: Narcisa (who married Santiago Muger), Teodora (Mrs. Francisco Rizal Mercado), Gregorio, Manuel and José. All were born in Manila, but lived in Kalamba, and they used the name Alonzo till that general change of names in 1850 when, with their mother, they adopted the name Realonda. This latter name has been said to be an allusion to royal blood in the family, but other indications suggest that it might have been a careless mistake made in writing by Rosa Realonda, whose name sometimes appears written as Redonda. There is a family Redondo (Redonda in its feminine form) Alonzo of Ilokano origin, the same stock as their traditions give for Mrs. Rizal's father, some of whose members were to be found in the neighborhood of Biñan and Pasay. One member of this family was akin in spirit to José Rizal, for he was fined twenty-five thousand pesos by the Supreme Court of the Philippine Islands for "contempt of religion." It appears that he put some original comparisons into a petition which sought to obtain justice from an inferior tribunal where, by the omission of the word "not" in copying, the clerk had reversed the court's decision but the judge refused to change the record.

Brigida de Quintos's death record, in Kalamba (1856), speaks of her as the daughter of Manuel de Quintos and Regina Ochoa.

The most obscure part of Rizal's family tree is the Ochoa branch, the family of the maternal grandmother, for all the archives,—church, land and court,—disappeared during the late disturbed conditions of which Cavite was the center. So one can only repeat what has been told by elderly people who have been found reliable in other accounts where the clews they gave could be compared with existing records.

The first of the family is said to have been Policarpio Ochoa, an employé of the Spanish customs house. Estanislao Manuel Ochoa was his son, with the blood of old Castile mingling with Chinese and Tagalog in his veins. He was part owner of the Hacienda of San Francisco de Malabon. One story says that somewhere in this family was a Mariquita Ochoa, of such beauty that she was known in Cavite, where was her home, as the Sampaguita (jasmine) of the Parian, or Chinese, quarter.

There was a Spanish nobleman also in Cavite in her time who had been deported for political reasons—probably for holding liberal opinions and for being thought to be favorable to English ideas. It is said that this particular "caja abierta" was a Marquis de Canete, and if so there is ground for the claim that he was of royal blood; at least some of his faroff ancestors had been related to a former ruling family of Spain.

Mariquita's mother knew the exile, since, according to the custom in Filipino families, she looked after the business interests of her husband. Curious to see the belle of whom he had heard so much, the Marquis made an excuse of doing business with the mother, and went to her home on an occasion when he knew that the mother was away. No one else was there to answer his knock and Mariquita, busied in making candy, could not in her confusion find a coconut shell to dip water for washing her hands from the large jar, and not to keep the visitor waiting, she answered the door as she was. Not only did her appearance realize the expectations of the Marquis, but the girl seemed equally attractive for her self-possessed manners and lively mind. The nobleman was charmed. On his way home he met a cart loaded with coconut dippers and he bought the entire lot and sent it as his first present.

After this the exile invented numerous excuses to call, till Mariquita's mother finally agreed to his union with her daughter. His political disability made him out of favor with the State church, the only place in which people could be married then, but Mariquita became what in English would be called a common-law wife. One of their children, José, had a tobacco factory and a slipper factory in Meisic, Manila, and was the especial protector of his younger sister, Regina, who became the wife of attorney
Manuel de Quintos. A sister of Regina was
Diega de Castro, who with another sister,

Luseria, sold "chorizos" (sausages) or "tiratira" (taffy candy), the first at a store and the second in their own home, but both in Cavite, according to the variations of one narrative.

A different account varies the time and omits the noble ancestor by saying that Regina was married unusually young to Manuel de Quintos to escape the attentions of the
Marquis. Another authority claims that

Regina was wedded to the lawyer in second marriage, being the widow of Facundo de Layva, the captain of the ship Hernando Magallanes, whose pilot, by the way, was Andrew Stewart, an Englishman.

It is certain that Regina Ochoa was of Spanish, Chinese and Tagalog ancestry, and it is recorded that she was the wife of Manuel de Quintos. Here we stop depending on memories, for in the restored burial register of Kalamba church in the entry of the funeral of Brigida de Quintos she is called "the daughter of Manuel de Quintos and Regina Ochoa."

Manuel de Quintos was an attorney of
Manila, graduated from Santo Tomás University, whose family were Chinese mestizos of Pangasinan. The lawyer's father, of the same name, had been municipal captain of Lingayan, and an uncle was leader of the Chinese mestizos in a protest they had made against the arbitrariness of their provincial governor. This petition for redress of grievances is preserved in the Supreme Court archives with "Joaquin de Quintos" well and boldly written at the head of the complainants' names, evidence of a culture and a courage that were equally uncommon in those days. Complaints under Spanish rule, no matter how well founded, meant trouble for the complainants; we must not forget that it was a vastly different thing from signing petitions or adhering to resolutions nowadays. Then the signers risked certainly great annoyance, sometimes imprisonment, and not infrequently death.

The home of Quintos had been in San Pedro Macati at the time of Captain Novales's uprising, the so-called "American revolt" in protest against the

Peninsulars sent out to supersede the Mexican officers who had remained loyal to Spain when the colony of their birth separated itself from the mother country. As little San Pedro Macati is charged with having originated the conspiracy, it is unlikely that it was concealed from the liberal lawyer, for attorneys were scarcer and held in higher esteem in those days.

The conservative element then, as later, did not often let drop any opportunity of purging the community of those who thought for themselves, by condemning them for crime unheard and undefended, whether they had been guilty of it or not.

All the branches of Mrs. Rizal's family were much richer than the relatives of her husband; there were numerous lawyers and priests among them—the old-time proof of social standing—and they were influential in the country.

There are several names of these related families that belong among the descendants of Lakandola, as traced by Mr. Luther Parker in his study of the Pampangan migration, and color is thereby given, so far as Rizal is concerned, to a proud boast that an old Pampangan lady of this descent makes for her family. She, who is exceedingly well posted upon her ancestry, ends the tracing of her lineage from Lakandola's time by asserting that the blood of that chief flowed in the veins of every Filipino who had the courage to stand forward as the champion of his people from the earliest days to the close of the Spanish régime. Lakandola, of course, belonged to the Mohammedan Sumatrans who emigrated to the Philippines only a few generations before Magellan's discovery.

To recall relatives of Mrs. Rizal who were in the professions may help to an understanding of the prominence of the family. Felix
Florentino, an uncle, was the first clerk of the Nueva Segovia (Vigan) court. A cousingerman, José Florentino, was a Philippine deputy in the Spanish Cortes, and a lawyer of note, as was also his brother, Manuel. Another relative, less near, was Clerk Reyes, of the Court of First Instance in Manila. The priest of Rosario, Vicar of Batangas Province, Father

Leyva, was a half-blood relation, and another priestly relative was Mrs. Rizal's paternal uncle, Father Alonzo. These were in the earlier days when professional men were scarcer. Father Almeida, of Santa Cruz Church, Manila, and Father Agustin Mendoz, his predecessor in the same church, and one of the sufferers in the Cavite trouble of '72—a deporté—were most distantly connected with the Rizal family. Another relative, of the Reyes connection, was in the Internal Revenue Service and had charge of Kalamba during the latter part of the eighteenth century.

Mrs. Rizal was baptized in Santa Cruz
Church, Manila, November 18, 1827, as Teodora Morales Alonzo, her godmother being a relative by marriage, Doña Maria Cristina. She was given an exceptionally good fundamental education by her gifted mother, and completed her training in Santa Rosa College, Manila, which was in the charge of Filipino sisters. Especially did the religious influence of her schooling manifest itself in her after life. Unfortunately there are no records in the institution, because it is said all the members of the Order who could read and write were needed for instruction and there was no one competent who had time for clerical work.

Brigida de Quintos had removed to the property in Kalamba which Lorenzo Alberto had transferred to her, and there as early as 1844 she is first mentioned as Brigida de Quintos, then as Brigida de Alonzo, and later as Brigida Realonda.

CHAPTER IV

Rizal's Early Childhood

JOSÉ PROTASIO RIZAL MERCADO Y
ALONZO REALONDA, the seventh child of
Francisco Engracio Rizal Mercado y
Alejandro and his wife, Teodora Morales Alonzo Realonda y Quintos, was born in Kalamba, June 19, 1861.

He was a typical Filipino, for few persons in this land of mixed blood could boast a greater mixture than his. Practically all the ethnic elements, perhaps even the Negrito in the far past, combined in his blood. All his ancestors, except the doubtful strain of the Negrito, had been immigrants to the Philippines, early Malays, and later Sumatrans, Chinese of prehistoric times and the refugees from the Tartar dominion, and Spaniards of old Castile and Valencia—representatives of all the various peoples who have blended to make the strength of the Philippine race.

Shortly before José's birth his family had built a pretentious new home in the center of Kalamba on a lot which Francisco Mercado had inherited from his brother. The house was destroyed before its usefulness had ceased, by the vindictiveness of those who hated the man-child that was born there. And later on the gratitude of a free people held the same spot sacred because there began that life consecrated to the Philippines and finally given for it, after preparing the way for the union of the various disunited Chinese mestizos, Spanish mestizos, and half a hundred dialectically distinguished "Indians" into the united people of the Philippines.

José was christened in the nearby church when three days old, and as two out-of-town bands happened to be in Kalamba for a local festival, music was a feature of the event. His godfather was Father Pedro Casañas, a Filipino priest of a Kalamba family, and the priest who christened him was also a Filipino, Father Rufino Collantes. Following is a translation of the record of Rizal's birth and baptism: "I, the undersigned parish priest of the town of Calamba, certify that from the investigation made with proper authority, for replacing the parish books which were burned September 28, 1862, to be found in Docket No. 1 of Baptisms, page 49, it appears by the sworn testimony of competent witnesses that JOSÉ RIZAL MERCADO is the legitimate son, and of lawful wedlock, of Don Francisco Rizal Mercado and Doña Teodora Realonda, having been baptized in this parish on the 22d day of June in the year 1861, by the parish priest, Rev. Rufino Collantes, Rev. Pedro Casañas being his godfather."—Witness my signature. (Signed) LEONCIO LOPEZ.

José Rizal's earliest training recalls the education of William and Alexander von Humboldt, those two nineteenth century Germans whose achievements for the prosperity of their fatherland and the advancement of humanity have caused them to be spoken of as the most remarkable pair of brothers that ever lived. He was not physically a strong child, but the direction of his first studies was by an unusually gifted mother, who succeeded, almost without the aid of books, in laying a foundation upon which the man placed an amount of wellmastered knowledge along many different lines that is truly marvelous, and this was done in so short a time that its brevity constitutes another wonder.

At three he learned his letters, having insisted upon being taught to read and being allowed to share the lessons of an elder sister. Immediately thereafter he was discovered with her story book, spelling out its words by the aid of the syllabary or "caton" which he had propped up before him and was using as one does a dictionary in a foreign language.

The little boy spent also much of his time in the church, which was conveniently near, but when the mother suggested that this might be an indication of religious inclination, his prompt response was that he liked to watch the people.

To how good purpose the small eyes and ears were used, the true-to-life types of the characters in "Noli Me Tangere" and "El Filibusterismo" testify.

Three uncles, brothers of the mother, concerned themselves with the intellectual, artistic and physical training of this promising nephew. The youngest, José, a teacher, looked after the regular lessons. The giant Manuel developed the physique of the youngster, until he had a supple body of silk and steel and was no longer a sickly lad, though he did not entirely lose his somewhat delicate looks. The more scholarly Gregorio saw that the child earned his candy money— trying to instill the idea into his mind that it was not the world's way that anything worth having should come without effort; he taught him also the value of rapidity in work, to think for himself, and to observe carefully and to picture what he saw.

Sometimes José would draw a bird flying without lifting pencil from the paper till the picture was finished. At other times it would be a horse running or a dog in chase, but it always must be something of which he had thought himself and the idea must not be overworked; there was no payment for what had been done often before. Thus he came to think for himself, ideas were suggested to him indirectly, so he was never a servile copyist, and he acquired the habit of speedy accomplishment.

Clay at first, then wax, was his favorite play material. From these he modeled birds and butterflies that came ever nearer to the originals in nature as the wise praise of the uncles called his attention to possibilities of improvement and encouraged him to further effort. This was the beginning of his nature study.

José had a pony and used to take long rides through all the surrounding country, so rich in picturesque scenery. Besides these horseback expeditions were excursions afoot; on the latter his companion was his big black dog, Usman. His father pretended to be fearful of some accident if dog and pony went together, so the boy had to choose between these favorites, and alternated walking and riding, just as Mr. Mercado had planned he should. The long pedestrian excursions of his European life, though spoken of as German and English habits, were merely continuations of this childhood custom. There were other playmates besides the dog and the horse, especially doves that lived in several houses about the Mercado home, and the lad was friend and defender of all the animals, birds, and even insects in the neighborhood. Had his childish sympathies been respected the family would have been strictly vegetarian in their diet.

At times José was permitted to spend the night in one of the curious little straw huts which La Laguna farmers put up during the harvest season, and the myths and legends of the region which he then heard interested him and were later made good use of in his writings.

Sleight-of-hand tricks were a favorite amusement, and he developed a dexterity which mystified the simple folk of the country. This diversion, and his proficiency in it, gave rise to that mysterious awe with which he was regarded by the common people of his home region; they ascribed to him supernatural powers, and refused to believe that he was really dead even after the tragedy of Bagumbayan.

Entertainment of the neighbors with magiclantern exhibitions was another frequent amusement, an ordinary lamp throwing its light on a common sheet serving as a screen. José's supple fingers twisted themselves into fantastic shapes, the enlarged shadows of which on the curtain bore resemblance to animals, and paper accessories were worked in to vary and enlarge the repertoire of action figures. The youthful showman was quite successful in catering to the public taste, and the knowledge he then gained proved valuable later in enabling him to approach his countrymen with books that held their attention and gave him the opportunity to tell them of shortcomings which it was necessary that they should correct.

Almost from babyhood he had a grown-up way about him, a sort of dignity that seemed to make him realize and respect the rights of others and unconsciously disposed his elders to reason with him, rather than scold him for his slight offenses. This habit grew, as reprimands were needed but once, and his grave promises of better behavior were faithfully kept when the explanation of why his conduct was wrong was once made clear to him. So the child came to be not an unwelcome companion even for adults, for he respected their moods and was never troublesome. A big influence in the formation of the child's character was his association with the parish priest of Kalamba, Father Leoncio Lopez.

The Kalamba church and convento, which were located across the way from the Rizal home, were constructed after the great earthquake of 1863, which demolished so many edifices throughout the central part of the Philippines.

The curate of Kalamba had a strong personality and was notable among the Filipino secular clergy of that day when responsibility had developed many creditable figures. An English writer of long residence in the Philippines, John Foreman, in his book on the Philippine Islands, describes how his first meeting with this priest impressed him, and tells us that subsequent acquaintance confirmed the early favorable opinion of one whom he considered remarkable for broad intelligence and sanity of view. Father Leoncío never deceived himself and his judgment was sound and clear, even when against the opinions and persons of whom he would have preferred to think differently. Probably José, through the priest's fondness for children and because he was well behaved and the son of friendly neighbors, was at first tolerated about the convento, the Philippine name for the priest's residence, but soon he became a welcome visitor for his own sake.

He never disturbed the priest's meditations when the old clergyman was studying out some difficult question, but was a keen observer, apparently none the less curious for his respectful reserve. Father Leoncío may have forgotten the age of his listener, or possibly was only thinking aloud, but he spoke of those matters which interested all thinking Filipinos and found a sympathetic, eager audience in the little boy, who at least gave close heed if he had at first no valuable comments to offer.

In time the child came to ask questions, and they were so sensible that careful explanation was given, and questions were not dismissed with the statement that these things were for grown-ups, a statement which so often repels the childish zeal for knowledge. Not many mature people in those days held so serious converse as the priest and his child friend, for fear of being overheard and reported, a danger which even then existed in the Philippines.

That the old Filipino priest of Rizal's novels owed something to the author's recollections of Father Leoncío is suggested by a chapter in "Noli Me Tangere." Ibarra, viewing Manila by moonlight on the first night after his return from Europe, recalls old memories and makes mention of the neighborhood of the Botanical Garden, just beyond which the friend and mentor of his youth had died. Father Leoncio Lopez died in Calle Concepción in that vicinity, which would seem to identify him in connection with that scene in the book, rather than numerous others whose names have been sometimes suggested.

Two writings of Rizal recall thoughts of his youthful days. One tells how he used to wander down along the lake shore and, looking across the waters, wonder about the people on the other side. Did they, too, he questioned, suffer injustice as the people of his home town did? Was the whip there used as freely, carelessly and unmercifully by the authorities? Had men and women also to be servile and hypocrites to live in peace over there? But among these thoughts, never once did it occur to him that at no distant day the conditions would be changed and, under a government that safeguarded the personal rights of the humblest of its citizens, the region that evoked his childhood wondering was to become part of a province bearing his own name in honor of his labors toward banishing servility and hypocrisy from the character of his countrymen.

The lake district of Central Luzon is one of the most historic regions in the Islands, the May-i probably of the twelfth century Chinese geographer. Here was the scene of the earliest Spanish missionary activity. On the south shore is Kalamba, birthplace of Doctor Rizal, with Biñan, the residence of his father's ancestors, to the northwest, and on the north shore the land to which reference is made above. Today this same region at the north bears the name of Rizal Province in his honor.

The other recollection of Rizal's youth is of his first reading lesson. He did not know Spanish and made bad work of the story of the "Foolish Butterfly," which his mother had selected, stumbling over the words and grouping them without regard to the sense. Finally Mrs. Rizal took the book from her son and read it herself, translating the tale into the familiar Tagalog used in their home. The moral is supposed to be obedience, and the young butterfly was burned and died because it disregarded the parental warning not to venture too close to the alluring flame. The reading lesson was in the evening and by the light of a coconut-oil lamp, and some moths were very appropriately fluttering about its cheerful blaze. The little boy watched them as his mother read and he missed the moral, for as the insects singed their wings and fluttered to their death in the flame he forgot their disobedience and found no warning in it for him. Rather he envied their fate and considered that the light was so fine a thing that it was worth dying for. Thus early did the notion that there are things worth more than life enter his head, though he could not foresee that he was to be himself a martyr and that the day of his death would before long be commemorated in his country to recall to his countrymen lessons as important to their national existence as his mother's precept was for his childish welfare.

When he was four the mystery of life's ending had been brought home to him by the death of a favorite little sister, and he shed the first tears of real sorrow, for until then he had only wept as children do when disappointed in getting their own way. It was the first of many griefs, but he quickly realized that life is a constant struggle and he learned to meet disappointments and sorrows with the tears in the heart and a smile on the lips, as he once advised a nephew to do.

At seven José made his first real journey; the family went to Antipolo with the host of pilgrims who in May visit the mountain shrine of Our Lady of Peace and Safe Travel. In the early Spanish days in Mexico she was the special patroness of voyages to America, especially while the galleon trade lasted; the statue was brought to Antipolo in 1672.

A print of the Virgin, a souvenir of this pilgrimage, was, according to the custom of those times, pasted inside José's wooden chest when he left home for school; later on it was preserved in an album and went with him in all his travels. Afterwards it faced Bougereau's splendid conception of the Christ-mother, as one who had herself thus suffered, consoling another mother grieving over the loss of a son. Many years afterwards Doctor Rizal was charged with having fallen away from religion, but he seems really rather to have experienced a deepening of the religious spirit which made the essentials of charity and kindness more important in his eyes than forms and ceremonies.

Yet Rizal practiced those forms prescribed for the individual even when debarred from church privileges. The lad doubtless got his idea of distinguishing between the sign and the substance from a well-worn book of explanations of the church ritual and symbolism "intended for the use of parish priests." It was found in his library, with Mrs. Rizal's name on the flyleaf. Much did he owe his mother, and his grateful recognition appears in his appreciative portrayal of maternal affection in his novels.

His parents were both religious, but in a different way. The father's religion was manifested in his charities; he used to keep on hand a fund, of which his wife had no account, for contributions to the necessitous and loans to the irresponsible. Mrs. Rizal attended to the business affairs and was more careful in her handling of money, though quite as charitably disposed. Her early training in Santa Rosa had taught her the habit of frequent prayer and she began early in the morning and continued till late in the evening, with frequent attendance in the church. Mr. Rizal did not forget his church duties, but was far from being so assiduous in his practice of them, and the discussions in the home frequently turned on the comparative value of words and deeds, discussions that were often given a humorous twist by the husband when he contrasted his wife's liberality in prayers with her more careful dispensing of money aid.

Not many homes in Kalamba were so well posted on events of the outside world, and the children constantly heard discussions of questions which other households either ignored or treated rather reservedly, for espionage was rampant even then in the Islands. Mrs. Rizal's literary training had given her an acquaintance with the better Spanish writers which benefited her children; she told them the classic tales in style adapted to their childish comprehension, so that when they grew older they found that many noted authors were old acquaintances. The Bible, too, played a large part in the home. Mrs. Rizal's copy was a Spanish translation of the Latin Vulgate, the version authorized by her Church but not common in the Islands then. Rizal's frequent references to Biblical personages and incidents are not paralleled in the writings of any contemporary Filipino author.

The frequent visitors to their home, the church, civil and military authorities, who found the spacious Rizal mansion a convenient resting place on their way to the health resort at Los Baños, brought something of the city, and a something not found by many residents even there, to the people of this village household. Oftentimes the house was filled, and the family would not turn away a guest of less rank for the sake of one of higher distinction, though that unsocial practice was frequently followed by persons who forgot their self-respect in toadying to rank.

Little José did not know Spanish very well, so far as conversational usage was concerned, but his mother tried to impress on him the beauty of the Spanish poets and encouraged him in essays at rhyming which finally grew into quite respectable poetical compositions. One of these was a drama in Tagalog which so pleased a municipal captain of the neighboring village of Paete, who happened to hear it while on a visit to Kalamba, that the youthful author was paid two pesos for the production. This was as much money as a field laborer in those days would have earned in half a month; although the family did not need the coin, the incident impressed them with the desirability of cultivating the boy's talent.

José was nine years old when he was sent to study in Biñan. His master there, Justiniano Aquino Cruz, was of the old school and Rizal has left a record of some of his maxims, such as "Spare the rod and spoil the child," "The letter enters with blood," and other similar indications of his heroic treatment of the unfortunates under his care. However, if he was a strict disciplinarian, Master Justiniano was also a conscientious instructor, and the boy had been only a few months under his care when the pupil was told that he knew as much as his master, and had better go to Manila to school. Truthful José repeated this conversation without the modification which modesty might have suggested, and his father responded rather vigorously to the idea and it was intimated that in the father's childhood pupils were not accustomed to say that they knew as much as their teachers. However, Master Justiniano corroborated the child's statement, so that preparations for José's going to Manila began to be made. This was in the Christmas vacation of 1871.

Biñan had been a valuable experience for young Rizal. There he had met a host of relatives and from them heard much of the past of his father's family. His maternal grandfather's great house was there, now inhabited by his mother's half-brother, a most interesting personage.

This uncle, José Alberto, had been educated in British India, spending eleven years in a Calcutta missionary school. This was the result of an acquaintance which his father had made with an English naval officer who visited the Philippines about 1820, the author of "An Englishman's Visit to the Philippines." Lorenzo Alberto, the grandfather, himself spoke English and had English associations. He had also liberal ideas and preferred the system under which the Philippines were represented in the Cortes and were treated not as a colony but as part of the homeland and its people were considered Spaniards.

The great Biñan bridge had been built under Lorenzo Alberto's supervision, and for services to the Spanish nation during the expedition to Cochin-China—probably liberal contributions of money—he had been granted the title of Knight of the American Order of Isabel the Catholic, but by the time this recognition reached him he had died, and the patent was made out to his son.

An episode well known in the village—its chief event, if one might judge from the conversation of the inhabitants—was a visit which a governor of Hongkong had made there when he was a guest in the home of Alberto. Many were the tales told of this distinguished Englishman, who was Sir John Bowring, the notable polyglot and translator into English of poetry in practically every one of the dialects of Europe. His achievements along this line had put him second or third among the linguists of the century. He was also interested in history, and mentioned in his Biñan visit that the Hakluyt Society, of which he was a Director, was then preparing to publish an exceedingly interesting account of the early Philippines that did more justice to its inhabitants than the regular Spanish historians. Here Rizal first heard of Morga, the historian, whose book he in after years made accessible to his countrymen. A desire to know other languages than his own also possessed him and he was eager to rival the achievements of Sir John Bowring.

In his book entitled "A Visit to the Philippine Islands," which was translated into Spanish by Mr. José del Pan, a liberal editor of Manila, Sir John Bowring gives the following account of his visit to Rizal's uncle:

"We reached Biñan before sunset .... First we passed between files of youths, then of maidens; and through a triumphal arch we reached the handsome dwelling of a rich mestizo, whom we found decorated with a Spanish order, which had been granted to his father before him. He spoke English, having been educated at Calcutta, and his house—a very large one—gave abundant evidence that he had not studied in vain the arts of domestic civilization. The furniture, the beds, the table, the cookery, were all in good taste, and the obvious sincerity of the kind reception added to its agreeableness. Great crowds were gathered together in the square which fronts the house of Don José Alberto."

The Philippines had just had a liberal governor, De la Torte, but even during this period of apparent liberalness there existed a confidential government order directing that all letters from Filipinos suspected of progressive ideas were to be opened in the post. This violation of the mails furnished the list of those who later suffered in the convenient insurrection of '72.

An agrarian trouble, the old disagreement between landlords and tenants, had culminated in an active outbreak which the government was unable to put down, and so it made terms by which, among other things,

the leader of the insurrection was established as chief of a new civil guard for the purpose of keeping order. Here again was another preparation for '72, for at that time the agreement was forgotten and the officer suffered punishment, in spite of the immunity he had been promised.

Religious troubles, too, were rife. The Jesuits had returned from exile shortly before, and were restricted to teaching work in those parishes in the missionary district where collections were few and danger was great. To make room for those whom they displaced the better parishes in the more thickly settled regions were taken from Filipino priests and turned over to members of the religious Orders. Naturally there was discontent. A confidential communication from the secular archbishop, Doctor Martinez, shows that he considered the Filipinos had ground for complaint, for he states that if the Filipinos were under a non-Catholic government like that of England they would receive fairer treatment than they were getting from their Spanish co-religionaries, and warns the home government that trouble will inevitably result if the discrimination against the natives of the country is continued.

The Jesuit method of education in their newly established "Ateneo Municipal" was a change from that in the former schools. It treated the Filipino as a Spaniard and made no distinctions between the races in the school dormitory. In the older institutions of Manila the Spanish students lived in the Spanish way and spoke their own language, but Filipinos were required to talk Latin, sleep on floor mats and eat with their hands from low tables. These Filipino customs obtained in the hamlets, but did not appeal to city lads who had become used to Spanish ways in their own homes and objected to departing from them in school. The disaffection thus created was among the educated class, who were best fitted to be leaders of their people in any dangerous insurrection against the government.

However, a change had to take place to meet the Jesuit competition, and in the rearrangement Filipino professors were given a larger share in the management of the schools. Notable among these was Father Burgos. He had earned his doctor's degree in two separate courses, was among the best educated in the capital and by far the most public-spirited and valiant of the Filipino priests.

He enlisted the interest of many of the older Filipino clergy and through their contributions subsidized a paper, El Eco Filipino, which spoke from the Filipino standpoint and answered the reflections which were the stock in trade of the conservative organ, for the reactionaries had an abusive journal just as they had had in 1821 and were to have in the later days.

Such were the conditions when José Rizal got ready to leave home for school in Manila, a departure which was delayed by the misfortunes of his mother. His only, and elder, brother, Paciano, had been a student in San José College in Manila for some years, and had regularly failed in passing his examinations because of his outspokenness against the evils of the country. Paciano was a great favorite with Doctor Burgos, in whose home he lived and for whom he acted as messenger and gobetween in the delicate negotiations of the propaganda which the doctor was carrying on.

In February of '72 all the dreams of a brighter and freer Philippines were crushed out in that enormous injustice which made the mutiny of a few soldiers and arsenal employés in Cavite the excuse for deporting, imprisoning, and even shooting those whose correspondence, opened during the previous year, had shown them to be discontented with the backward conditions in the Philippines.

Doctor Burgos, just as he had been nominated to a higher post in the Church, was the chief victim. Father Gomez, an old man, noted for charity, was another, and the third was Father
Zamora. A reference in a letter of his to "powder," which was his way of saying money, was distorted into a dangerous significance, in spite of the fact that the letter was merely an invitation to a gambling game. The trial was a farce, the informer was garroted just when he was on the point of complaining that he was not receiving the pardon and payment which he had been promised for his services in convicting the others. The whole

affair had an ugly look, and the way it was hushed up did not add to the confidence of the people in the justice of the proceedings. The Islands were then placed under military law and remained so for many years.

Father Burgos's dying advice to Filipinos was for them to be educated abroad, preferably outside of Spain, but if they could do no better, at least go to the Peninsula. He urged that through education only could progress be hoped for. In one of his speeches he had warned the Spanish government that continued oppressive measures would drive the Filipinos from their allegiance and make them wish to become subjects of a freer power, suggesting England, whose possessions surrounded the Islands.

Doctor Burgos's idea of England as a hope for the Philippines was borne out by the interest which the British newspapers of Hongkong took in Philippine affairs. They gave accounts of the troubles and picked flaws in the garbled reports which the officials sent abroad.

Some zealous but unthinking reactionary at this time conceived the idea of publishing a book somewhat similar to that which had been gotten out against the Constitution of Cadiz. "Captain Juan" was its name; it was in catechism form, and told of an old municipal captain who deserved to be honored because he was so submissively subservient to all constituted authority. He tries to distinguish between different kinds of liberty, and the especial attention which he devotes to America shows how live a topic the great republic was at that time in the Islands. This interest is explained by the fact that an American company had just then received a grant of the northern part of Borneo, later British North Borneo, for a trading company.
It was believed that the United States had designs on the Archipelago because of treaties which had been negotiated with the Sultan of Sulu and certain American commercial interests in the Far East, which were then rather important.

Americans, too, had become known in the Philippines through a soldier of fortune who had helped out the Chinese government in suppressing the rebellion in the neighborhood of Shanghai. "General" F. T. Ward, from Massachusetts, organized an army of deserters from European ships, but their lack of discipline made them undesirable soldiers, and so he disbanded the force. He then gathered a regiment of Manila men, as the Filipinos usually found as quartermasters on all ships sailing in the East were then called. With the aid of some other Americans these troops were disciplined and drilled into such efficiency that the men came to have the title among the Chinese of the "Ever-Victorious" army, because of the almost unbroken series of successes which they had experienced. A partial explanation, possibly, of their fighting so well is that they were paid only when they won.

The high praise given the Filipinos at this time was in contrast to the disparagement made of their efforts in Indo-China, where in reality they had done the fighting rather than their Spanish officers. When a Spaniard in the Philippines quoted of the Filipino their customary saying, "Poor soldier, worse sacristan," the Filipinos dared make no open reply, but they consoled themselves with remembering the flattering comments of "General" Ward and the favorable opinion of Archbishop Martinez.

References to Filipino military capacity were banned by the censors and the archbishop's communication had been confidential, but both became known, for despotisms drive its victims to stealth and to methods which would not be considered creditable under freer conditions.

CHAPTER V

Jagor's Prophecy

RIZAL'S first home in Manila was in a nipa house with Manuel Hidalgo, later to be his brother-in-law, in Calle Espeleta, a street named for a former Filipino priest who had risen to be bishop and governor-general. This spot is now marked with a tablet which gives the date of his coming as the latter part of February, 1872.

Rizal's own recollections speak of June as being the date of the formal beginning of his studies in Manila. First he went to San Juan de Letran and took an examination in the Catechism. Then he went back to Kalamba and in July passed into the Ateneo, possibly because of the more favorable conditions under which the pupils were admitted, receiving credit for work in arithmetic, which in the other school, it is said, he would have had to restudy. This perhaps accounts for the credit shown in the scholastic year 1871-72. Until his fourth year Rizal was an externe, as those residing outside of the school dormitory were then called. The Ateneo was very popular and so great was the eagerness to enter it that the waiting list was long and two or three years' delay was not at all uncommon.

There is a little uncertainty about this period; some writers have gone so far as to give recollections of childhood incidents of which Rizal was the hero while he lived in the house of Doctor Burgos, but the family deny that he was ever in this home, and say that he has been confused with his brother Paciano.

The greatest influence upon Rizal during this period was the sense of Spanish judicial injustice in the legal persecutions of his mother, who, though innocent, for two years was treated as a criminal and held in prison.

Much of the story is not necessary for this narrative, but the mother's troubles had their beginning in the attempted revenge of a lieutenant of the Civil Guard, one of a body of Spaniards who were no credit to the mother country and whom Rizal never lost opportunity in his writings of painting in their true colors. This official had been in the habit of having his horse fed at the Mercado home when he visited their town from his station in Biñan, but once there was a scarcity of fodder and Mr. Mercado insisted that his own stock was entitled to care before he could extend hospitality to strangers. This the official bitterly resented. His opportunity for revenge soon came, and was not overlooked. A disagreement between José Alberto, the mother's brother in Biñan, and his wife, also his cousin, to whom he had been married when they were both quite young, led to sensational charges which a discreet officer would have investigated and would assuredly have then realized to be unfounded. Instead the lieutenant accepted the most ridiculous statements, brought charges of attempted murder against Alberto and his sister, Mrs. Rizal, and evidently figured that he would be able to extort money from the rich man and gratify his revenge at the same time.

Now comes a disgruntled judge, who had not received the attention at the Mercado home which he thought his dignity demanded. Out of revenge he ordered Mrs. Rizal to be conducted at once to the provincial prison, not in the usual way by boat, but, to cause her greater annoyance, afoot around the lake. It was a long journey from Kalamba to Santa Cruz, and the first evening the guard and his prisoner came to a village where there was a festival in progress. Mrs. Rizal was well known and was welcomed in the home of one of the prominent families. The festivities were at their height when the judge, who had been on horseback and so had reached the town earlier, heard that the prisoner, instead of being in the village calaboose, was a guest of honor and apparently not suffering the annoyance to which he had intended to subject her. He strode to the house, and, not content to knock, broke in the door, splintered his cane on the poor constable's head, and then exhausted himself beating the owner of the house.

These proceedings were revealed in a charge of prejudice which Mrs. Rizal's lawyers urged against the judge who at the same time was the one who decided the case and also the prosecutor. The Supreme Court agreed that her contention was correct and directed that she be discharged from custody. To this order the judge paid due respect and ordered her release, but he said that the accusation of unfairness against him was contempt of court, and gave her a longer sentence under this charge than the previous one from which she had just been absolved. After some delay the Supreme Court heard of this affair and decided that the judge was right. But, because Mrs. Rizal had been longer in prison awaiting trial than the sentence, they dated back her imprisonment, and again ordered her release. Here the record gets a little confused because it is concerned with a story that her brother had sixteen thousand pesos concealed in his cell, and everybody, from the Supreme Court down, seemed interested in trying to locate the money.

While the officials were looking for his sack of gold, Alberto gave a power of attorney to an overintelligent lawyer who worded his authority so that it gave him the right to do everything which his principal himself could have done "personally, legally and ecclesiastically." From some source outside, but not from the brother, the attorney heard that Mrs. Rizal had had money belonging to Alberto, for in the extensive sugarpurchasing business which she carried on she handled large sums and frequently borrowed as much as five thousand pesos from this brother. Anxious to get his hands on money, he instituted a charge of theft against her, under his power of attorney and acting in the name of his principal. Mrs. Rizal's attorney demurred to such a charge being made without the man who had lent the money being at all consulted, and held that a power of attorney did not warrant such an action. In time the intelligent Supreme Court heard this case and decided that it should go to trial; but later, when the attorney, acting for his principal, wanted to testify for him under the power of attorney, they seem to have reached their limit, for they disapproved of that proposal.

Anyone who cares to know just how ridiculous and inconsistent the judicial system of the Philippines then was would do well to try to unravel the mixed details of the half dozen charges, ranging from cruelty through theft to murder, which were made against Mrs. Rizal without a shadow of evidence. One case was trumped up as soon as another was finished, and possibly the affair would have dragged on till the end of the Spanish administration had not her little daughter danced before the Governor-General once when he was traveling through the country, won his approval, and when he asked what favor he could do for her, presented a petition for her mother's release. In this way, which recalls the customs of primitive nations, Mrs. Rizal finally was enabled to return to her home.

Doctor Rizal tells us that it was then that he first began to lose confidence in mankind. A story of a school companion, that when Rizal recalled this incident the red came into his eyes, probably has about the same foundation as the frequent stories of his weeping with emotion upon other people's shoulders when advised of momentous changes in his life.

Doctor Rizal did not have these Spanish ways, and the narrators are merely speaking of what other Spaniards would have done, for selfrestraint and freedom from exhibitions of emotion were among his most prominent characteristics.

Some time during Rizal's early years of school came his first success in painting. It was the occasion of a festival in Kalamba; just at the last moment an important banner was accidentally damaged and there was not time to send to Manila for another. A hasty consultation was held among the village authorities, and one councilman suggested that José Rizal had shown considerable skill with the brush and possibly he could paint something that would pass. The gobernadorcillo proceeded to the lad's home and explained the need. Rizal promptly went to work, under the official's direction, and speedily produced a painting which the delighted municipal executive declared was better than the expensive banner bought in Manila. The achievement was explained to all the participants in the festival and young José was the hero of the occasion.

During intervals of school work Rizal found time to continue his modeling in clay which he procured from the brickyard of a cousin at San Pedro Macati.

Rizal's uncle, José Alberto, had played a considerable part in his political education. He was influential with the Regency in Spain, which succeeded Queen Isabel when that sovereign became too malodorous to be longer tolerated, and he was the personal friend of the Regent, General Prim, whose motto, "More liberal today than yesterday, more liberal tomorrow than today," he was fond of quoting. He was present in Madrid at the time of General Prim's assassination and often told of how this wise patriot, recognizing the unpreparedness of the Spanish people for a republic, opposed the efforts for what would, he knew, result in as disastrous a failure as had been France's first effort, and how he lost his life through his desire to follow the safer course of proceeding gradually through the preparatory stage of a constitutional monarchy. Alberto was made by him a Knight of the Order of Carlos III, and, after Prim's death, was created by King Amadeo a Knight Commander, the step higher in the Order of Isabel the Catholic.

Events proved Prim's wisdom, as Alberto was careful to observe, for King Amadeo was soon convinced of the unfitness of his people for even a constitutional monarchy, told them so, resigned his throne, and bade them farewell. Then came a republic marked by excesses such as even the worst monarch had not committed; among them the dreadful massacre of the members of the filibustering party on the steamer Virginius in Cuba, which would have caused war with the United States had not the Americans been deluded into the idea that they were dealing with a sister republic. America and Switzerland had been the only nations which had recognized Spain's new form of government. Prim sought an alliance with America, for he claimed that Spain should be linked with a country which would buy Spanish goods and to which Spain could send her products. France, with whom the Bourbons wished to be allied, was a competitor along Spain's own lines.

During the earlier disturbances in Spain a party of Carlists were sent to the Philippine Islands; they were welcomed by the reactionary Spaniards, for devotion to King Carlos had been their characteristic ever since the days when Queen Isabel had taken the throne that in their opinion belonged to the heir in the male line. Rizal frequently makes mention of this disloyalty to the ruler of Spain on the part of those who claimed to be most devoted Spaniards.

Along with the stories of these troubles which Rizal heard during his school days in Manila were reports of how these exiles had established themselves in foreign cities, Basa in Hongkong, Regidor in London, and Tavera in Paris. At their homes in these cities they gave a warm welcome to such Filipinos as traveled abroad and they were always ready to act as

guardians for Filipino students who wished to study in their cities, Many availed themselves of these opportunities and it came to be an ambition among those in the Islands to get an education which they believed was better than that which Spain afforded. There was some ground for such a belief, because many of the most prominent successful men of Spanish and Philippine birth were men whose education had been foreign. A wellknown instance in Manila was the architect Roxas, father of the present Alcalde of
Manila, who learned his profession in England and was almost the only notable builder in Manila during his lifetime.

Paciano Rizal, José's elder brother, had retired from Manila on the death of Doctor Burgos and devoted himself to farming; in some ways, perhaps, his career suggested the character of Tasio, the philosopher of "Noli Me Tangere." He was careful to see that his younger brother was familiar with the liberal literature with which he had become acquainted through Doctor Burgos.

The first foreign book read by Rizal, in a Spanish translation, was Dumas's great novel, "The Count of Monte Cristo," and the story of the wrongs suffered by the prisoner of the Château d'If recalled the injustice done his mother. Then came the book which had greatest influence upon the young man's career; this was a Spanish translation of Jagor's "Travels in the Philippines," the observations of a German naturalist who had visited the Islands some fifteen years before. This latter book, among other comments, suggested that it was the fate of the North American republic to develop and bring to their highest prosperity the lands which Spain had conquered and Christianized with sword and cross. Sooner or later, this German writer believed, the Philippine Islands could no more escape this American influence than had the countries on the mainland, and expressed the hope that one day the Philippines would succumb to the same influence; he felt, however, that it was desirable first for the Islanders to become better able to meet the strong competition of the vigorous young people of the New World, for under Spain the Philippines had dreamed away its past.

The exact title of the book is "Travels | in the | Philippines. | By F. Jagor. | With numerous illustrations and a Map | London: | Chapman and Hall, 193, Piccadilly. | 1875." The title of the Spanish translation reads, "Viajes | por | Filipinas | de F. Jagor | Traducidos del Alemán | por S. Vidal y Soler | Ingeniero de Montes | Edición illustrada con numerosos grabados | Madrid: Imprenta, Estereopidea y Galvanoplastia de Ariban y Ca. | (Sucesores de Rivadencyra) | Impresores de Camara de S. M. | Calle del Duque de Osuna, núm 3. 1875," The following extract from the book will show how marvelously the author anticipated events that have now become history:

"With the altered condition of things, however, all this has disappeared. The colony can no longer be kept secluded from the world. Every facility afforded for commercial intercourse is a blow to the old system, and a great step made in the direction of broad and liberal reforms. The more foreign capital and foreign ideas and customs are introduced, increasing the prosperity, enlightenment, and self-esteem of the population, the more impatiently will the existing evils be endured.

England can and does open her possessions unconcernedly to the world. The British colonies are united to the mother country by the bond of mutual advantage, viz., the produce of raw material by means of English capital, and the exchange of the same for English manufactures. The wealth of England is so great, the organization of her commerce with the world so complete, that nearly all the foreigners even in the British possessions are for the most part agents for English business houses, which would scarcely be affected, at least to any marked extent, by a political dismemberment. It is entirely different with Spain, which possesses the colony as an inherited property, and without the power of turning it to any useful account.

Government monopolies rigorously maintained, insolent disregard and neglect of the half-castes and powerful creoles, and the example of the United States, were the chief reasons of the downfall of the American possessions. The same causes threaten ruin to the Philippines; but of the monopolies I have said enough.

Half-castes and creoles, it is true are not, as they formerly were in America, excluded from all orificial appointments; but they feel deeply hurt and injured through the crowds of place-hunters which the frequent changes of Ministers send to Manilla. The influence, also, of the American element is at least visible on the horizon, and will be more noticeable when the relations increase between the two countries. At present they are very slender. The trade in the meantime follows in its old channels to England and to the Atlantic ports of the United States. Nevertheless, whoever desires to form an opinion upon the future history of the Philippines, must not consider simply their relations to Spain, but must have regard to the prodigious changes which a few decades produce on either side of our planet.

For the first time in the history of the world the mighty powers on both sides of the ocean have commenced to enter upon a direct intercourse with one another—Russia, which alone is larger than any two other parts of the earth; China, which contains within its own boundaries a third of the population of the world; and America, with ground under cultivation nearly sufficient to feed treble the total population of the earth. Russia's further rôle in the Pacific Ocean is not to be estimated at present.

The trade between the two other great powers will therefore be presumably all the heavier, as the rectification of the pressing need of human labour on the one side, and of the corresponding overplus on the other, will fall to them.

"The world of the ancients was confined to the shores of the Mediterranean; and the Atlantic and Indian Oceans sufficed at one time for our traffic. When first the shores of the Pacific re-echoed with the sounds of active commerce, the trade of the world and the history of the world may be really said to have begun. A start in that direction has been made; whereas not so very long ago the immense ocean was one wide waste of waters, traversed from both points only once a year. From 1603 to 1769 scarcely a ship had ever visited California, that wonderful country which, twenty-five years ago, with the exception of a few places on the coast, was an unknown wilderness, but which is now covered with flourishing and prosperous towns and cities, divided from sea to sea by a railway, and its capital already ranking the third of the seaports of the Union; even at this early stage of its existence a central point of the world's commerce, and apparently destined, by the proposed junction of the great oceans, to play a most important part in the future.

In proportion as the navigation of the west coast of America extends the influence of the American element over the South Sea, the captivating, magic power which the great republic exercises over the Spanish colonies[1] will not fail to make itself felt also in the Philippines. The Americans are evidently destined to bring to a full development the germs originated by the Spaniards. As conquerors of modern times, they pursue their road to victory with the assistance of the pioneer's axe and plough, representing an age of peace and commercial prosperity in contrast to that bygone and chivalrous age whose champions were upheld by the cross and protected by the sword.

A considerable portion of Spanish America already belongs to the United States, and has since attained an importance which could not possibly have been anticipated either under the Spanish Government or during the anarchy which followed. With regard to permanence, the Spanish system cannot for a moment be compared with that of America. While each of the colonies, in order to favour a privileged class by immediate gains, exhausted still more the already enfeebled population of the metropolis by the withdrawal of the best of its ability, America, on the contrary, has attracted to itself from all countries the most energetic element, which, once on its soil and, freed from all fetters, restlessly progressing, has extended its power and influence still further and further. The Philippines will escape the action of the two great neighbouring powers all the less for the fact that neither they nor their metropolis find their condition of a stable and well-balanced nature.

It seems to be desirable for the natives that the above-mentioned views should not speedily become accomplished facts, because their education and training hitherto have not been of a nature to prepare them successfully to compete with either of the other two energetic, creative, and progressive nations. They have, in truth, dreamed away their best days."

This prophecy of Jagor's made a deep impression upon Rizal and seems to furnish the explanation of his life work. Henceforth it was his ambition to arouse his countrymen to prepare themselves for a freer state. He dedicated himself to the work which Doctor Jagor had indicated as necessary. It seems beyond question that Doctor Rizal, as early as 1876, believed that America would sometime come to the Philippines, and wished to prepare his countrymen for the changed conditions that would then have to be met. Many little incidents in his later life confirm this view: his eagerness to buy expensive books on the United States, such as his early purchase in Barcelona of two different "Lives of the Presidents of the United States"; his study of the country in his travel across it from San Francisco to New York; the reference in "The Philippines in a Hundred Years"; and the studies of the English Revolution and other Anglo-Saxon influences which culminated in the foundation of the United States of America.

Besides the interest he took in clay modeling, to which reference has already been made, Rizal was expert in carving. When first in the Ateneo he had carved an image of the Virgin of such grace and beauty that one of the Fathers asked him to try an image of the Sacred Heart. Rizal complied, and produced the carving that played so important a part in his future life. The Jesuit Father had intended to take the image with him to Spain, but in some way it was left behind and the schoolboys put it up on the door of their dormitory. There it remained for nearly twenty years, constantly reminding the many lads who passed in and out of the one who teachers and pupils alike agreed was the greatest of all their number, for Rizal during these years was the schoolboy hero of the Ateneo, and from the Ateneo came the men who were most largely concerned in making the New Philippines. The image itself is of batikulin, an easily carved wood, and shows considerable skill when one remembers that an ordinary pocketknife was the simple instrument

used in its manufacture. It was recalled to Rizal's memory when he visited the Ateneo upon his first return from Spain and was forbidden the house by the Jesuits because of his alleged apostasy, and again in the chapel of Fort Santiago, where it played an important part in what was called his conversion.

The proficiency he attained in the art of clay modeling is evidenced by many of the examples illustrated in this volume. They not only indicate an astonishing versatility, but they reveal his very characteristic method of working—a characteristic based on his constant desire to adapt the best things he found abroad to the conditions of his own country. The same characteristic appears also in most of his literary work, and in it there is no servile imitation; it is careful and studied selection, adaptation and combination. For example, the composition of a steel engraving in a French art journal suggested his model in clay of a Philippine wild boar; the head of the subject in a painting in the Luxembourg Gallery and the rest of a figure in an engraving in a newspaper are combined in a statuette he modeled in Brussels and sent, in May, 1890, to Valentina Ventura in place of a letter; a clipping from a newspaper cut is also adapted for his model of "The Vengeance of the Harem"; and as evidence of his facility of expressing himself in this medium, his clay modeling of a Dapitan woman may be cited. One day while in exile he saw a native woman clearing up the street in front of her home preparatory to a festival; the movements and the attitudes of the figure were so thoroughly typical and so impressed themselves on his mind that he worked out this statuette from memory.

In a literary way Rizal's first pretentious effort was a melodrama in one act and in verse, entitled "Junta al Pasig" (Beside the Pasig), a play in honor of the Virgin, which was given in the Ateneo to the great edification of a considerable audience, who were enthusiastic in their praise and hearty in their applause, but the young author neither saw the play nor paid any attention to the manner of its reception, for he was downstairs, intent on his own diversions and heedless of what was going on above.

Thursday was the school holiday in those days, and Rizal usually spent the time at the Convent of La Concordia, where his youngest sister, Soledad, was a boarder. He was a great friend of the little one and a welcome visitor in the Convent; he used to draw pictures for her edification, sometimes teasing her by making her own portrait, to which he gave exaggerated ears to indicate her curiosity. Then he wrote short satirical skits, such as the following, which in English doggerel quite matches its Spanish original:

"The girls of Concordia College
Go dressed in the latest of styles— Bangs high on their foreheads for knowledge—
But hungry their grins and their smiles!"

Some of these girls made an impression upon José, and one of his diary entries of this time tells of his rude awakening when a girl, some years his elder, who had laughingly accepted his boyish adoration, informed him that she was to marry a relative of his, and he speaks of the heartpang with which he watched the carromata that carried her from his sight to her wedding.

José was a great reader, and the newspapers were giving much attention to the World's Fair in Philadelphia which commemorated the first centennial of American independence, and published numerous cuts illustrating various interesting phases of American life. Possibly as a reaction from the former disparagement of things American, the sentiment in the Philippines was then very friendly. There was one long account of the presentation of a Spanish banner to a Spanish commission in Philadelphia, and the newspapers, in speaking of the wonderful progress which the United States had made, recalled the early Spanish alliance and referred to the fact that, had it not been for the discoveries of the Spaniards, their new land would not have been known to Europe.

Rizal during his last two years in the Ateneo was a boarder. Throughout his entire course he had been the winner of most of the prizes. Upon receiving his Bachelor of Arts diploma he entered the University of Santo Tomás; in the first year he studied the course in philosophy and in the second year began to specialize in medicine.

The Ateneo course of study was a good deal like that of our present high school, though not so thorough nor so advanced. Still, the method of instruction which has made Jesuit education notable in all parts of the world carried on the good work which the mother's training had begun. The system required the explanation of the morrow's lesson, questioning on the lesson of the day and a review of the previous day's work. This, with the attention given to the classics, developed and quickened faculties which gave Rizal a remarkable power of assimilating knowledge of all kinds for future use.

The story is told that Rizal was undecided as to his career, and wrote to the rector of the Ateneo for advice; but the Jesuit was then in the interior of Mindanao, and by the time the answer, suggesting that he should devote himself to agriculture, was received, he had already made his choice. However, Rizal did continue the study of agriculture, besides specializing in medicine, carrying on double work as he took the course in the Ateneo which led to the degree of land surveyor and agricultural expert. This work was completed before he had reached the age fixed by law, so that he could not then receive his diploma, which was not delivered to him until he had attained the age of twenty-one years.

In the "Life" of Rizal published in Barcelona after his death a brilliant picture is painted of how Rizal might have followed the advice of the rector of the Ateneo, and have lived a long, useful and honorable life as a farmer and gobernadorcillo of his home town, respected by the

Spaniards, looked up to by his countrymen and filling an humble but safe lot in life. Today one can hardly feel that such a career would have been suited to the man or regret that events took the course they did.

Poetry was highly esteemed in the Ateneo, and Rizal frequently made essays in verse, often carrying his compositions to Kalamba for his mother's criticisms and suggestions. The writings of the Spanish poet Zorilla were making a deep impression upon him at this time, and while his schoolmates seemed to have been more interested in their warlike features, José appears to have gained from them an understanding of how Zorilla sought to restore the Spanish people to their former dignity, rousing their pride through recalling the heroic events in their past history. Some of the passages in the melodrama, "Junta al Pasig," already described, were evidently influenced by his study of Zorilla; the fierce denunciation of Spain which is there put in the mouth of Satan expresses, no doubt, the real sentiments of Rizal.

In 1877 a society known as the Liceo
Literario-Artistica (Lyceum of Art and Literature) offered a prize for the best poem by a native. The winner was Rizal with the following verses, "Al Juventud Filipino" (To the Philippine Youth). The prize was a silver pen, feather-shaped and with a gold ribbon running through it.

To the Philippine Youth

Theme: "Growth"

(Translation by Charles Derbyshire)

Hold high the brow serene,
O youth, where now you stand;
Let the bright sheen Of your grace be seen, Fair hope
of my fatherland!

Come now, thou genius grand,
And bring down inspiration;

With thy mighty hand, Swifter than the wind's volation, Raise the eager mind to higher station.

Come down with pleasing light

Of art and science to the fight,
O youth, and there untie
The chains that heavy lie, Your spirit free to blight.

See how in flaming zone
Amid the shadows thrown,
The Spaniard's holy hand
A crown's resplendent band Proffers to this Indian land.

Thou, who now wouldst rise
On wings of rich emprise,
Seeking from Olympian skies
Songs of sweetest strain,
Softer than ambrosial rain;

Thou, whose voice divine
Rivals Philomel's refrain,
And with varied line
Through the night benign
Frees mortality from pain;

Thou, who by sharp strife
Wakest thy mind to life;
And the memory bright
Of thy genius' light
Makest immortal in its strength;

And thou, in accents clear of Phoebus, to Apells dear; Or by the brush's magic art
Takest from nature's store a part,
To fix it on the simple canvas' length;

Go forth, and then the sacred fire
Of thy genius to the laurel may aspire; To spread around the fame,
And in victory acclaim,
Through wider spheres the human name.

Day, O happy day,
Fair Filipinas, for thy land!
So bless the Power today
That places in thy way
This favor and this fortune grand.

The next competition at the Liceo was in honor of the fourth centennial of the death of Cervantes; it was open to both Filipinos and Spaniards, and there was a dispute as to the winner of the prize. It is hard to figure out just what really happened; the newspapers speak of Rizal as winning the first prize, but his certificate says second, and there seems to have been some sort of compromise by which a Spaniard who was second was put at the head. Newspapers, of course, were then closely censored, but the liberal La Oceania contains a number of veiled allusions to medical poets, suggesting that for the good of humanity they should not be permitted to waste their time in verse-making. One reference quotes the title of Rizal's first poem in saying that it was giving a word of advice "To the Philippine Youth," and there are other indications that for some considerable time the outcome of this contest was a very live topic in the city of Manila.

Rizal's poem was an allegory, "The Council of the Gods"—"El consejo de los Dioses." It was an exceedingly artistic appreciation of the chief figure in Spanish literature. The rector of the Ateneo had assisted his former student by securing for him needed books, and though Rizal was at that time a student in Santo Tomás, the rivalries were such that he was still ranked with the pupils of the Jesuits and his success was a corresponding source of elation to the Ateneo pupils and alumni.
Some people have stated that Father Evaristo

Arias, a notably brilliant writer of the Dominicans, was a competitor, a version I once published, but investigation shows that this was a mistake. However, sentiment in the University against Rizal grew, until matters became so unpleasant that he felt it time to follow the advice of Father Burgos and continue his education outside of the Islands.

Just before this incident Rizal had been the victim of a brutal assault in Kalamba; one night when he was passing the barracks of the Civil Guard he noted in the darkness a large body, but did not recognize who it was, and passed without any attention to it. It turned out that the large body was a lieutenant of the Civil Guard, and, without warning or word of any kind, he drew his sword and wounded Rizal in the back. Rizal complained of this outrage to the authorities and tried several times, without success, to see the GovernorGeneral. Finally he had to recognize that there was no redress for him. By May of 1882 Rizal had made up his mind to set sail for Europe, and his brother, Paciano, equipped him with seven hundred pesos for the journey, while his sister, Saturnina, intrusted to him a valuable diamond ring which might prove a resource in time of emergency.

José had gone to Kalamba to attend a festival there, when Mr. Hidalgo, from Manila, notified him that his boat was ready to sail. The telegram, asking his immediate return to the city, was couched in the form of advice of the condition of a patient, and the name of the steamer, Salvadora, by a play on words, was used in the sense of "May save her life." Rizal had previously requested of Mr. Ramirez, of the Puerta del Sol store, letters of introduction to an Englishman, formerly in the Philippines, who was then living in Paris. He said nothing more of his intentions, but on his last night in the city, with his younger sister as companion, he drove all through the walled city and its suburbs, changing horses twice in the five hours of his farewell. The next morning he embarked on the steamer, and there yet remains the sketch which he made of his last view of the city, showing its waterfront as it appeared from the departing steamer. To leave town it was necessary to have a passport; his was in the name of José Mercado, and had been secured by a distant relative of his who lived in the Santa Cruz district.

After five days' journey the little steamer reached the English colony of Singapore. There Rizal saw a modern city for the first time. He was intensely interested in the improvements. Especially did the assured position of the natives, confident in their rights and not fearful of the authorities, arouse his admiration. Great was the contrast between the fear of their rulers shown by the Filipinos and the confidence which the natives of Singapore seemed to have in their government.

At Singapore, Rizal transferred to a French mail Steamer and seems to have had an interesting time making himself understood on board. He had studied some French in his Ateneo course, writing an ode which gained honors, but when he attempted to speak the language he was not successful in making Frenchmen understand him. So he resorted to a mixed system of his own, sometimes using Latin words and making the changes which regularly would have occurred, and when words failed, making signs, and in extreme cases drawing pictures of what he wanted. This versatility with the pencil, for many of his offhand sketches had humorous touches that almost carried them into the cartoon class, interested officers and passengers, so that the young student had the freedom of the ship and a voyage far from tedious.

The passage of the Suez Canal, a glimpse of Egypt, Aden, where East and West meet, and the Italian city of Naples, with its historic castle, were the features of the trip which most impressed him.

CHAPTER VI

The Period of Preparation

Rizal disembarked at Marseilles, saw a little of that famous port, and then went by rail to Barcelona, crossing the Pyrenees, the desolate ruggedness of which contrasted with the picturesque luxuriance of his tropical home, and remained a day at the frontier town of Port-Bou. The customary Spanish disregard of tourists compared very unfavorably with the courteous attention which he had remarked on his arrival at Marseilles, for the custom house officers on the Spanish frontier rather reminded him of the class of employes found in Manila.

At Barcelona he met many who had been his schoolmates in the Ateneo and others to whom he was known by name. It was the custom of the Filipino students there to hold reunions every other Sunday at the café, for their limited resources did not permit the daily visits which were the Spanish custom. In honor of the new arrival a special gathering occurred in a favorite café in Plaza de Catalonia. The characteristics of the Spaniards and the features of Barcelona were all described for Rizal's benefit, and he had to answer a host of questions about the changes which had occurred in Manila. Most of his answers were to the effect that old defects had not yet been remedied nor incompetent officials supplanted, and he gave a rather hopeless view of the future of their country. Somewhat in this gloomy mood, he wrote home for a newly established Tagalog newspaper of Manila, his views of "Love of country," an article not so optimistic as most of his later writings.

In Barcelona he remained but a short time, long enough, however, to see the historic sights around that city, which was established by Hannibal, had numbered many noted
Romans among its residents, and in later days was the scene of the return of Columbus from his voyages in the New World, bringing with him samples of Redskins, birds and other novel products of the unknown country. Then there were the magnificent boulevards, the handsome dwellings, the interest which the citizens took in adorning their city and the pride in the results, and above all, the disgust at all things Spanish and the loyalty to Catalonia, rather than to the "motherfatherland."

The Catalan was the most progressive type in Spain, but he had no love for his compatriots, was ever complaining of their "mañana" habits and of the evils that were bound to exist in a country where Church and State were so inextricably intermingled. Many Catalans were avowedly republicans. Signs might be seen on the outside of buildings telling of the location of republican clubs, unpopular officials were hooted in the streets, the newspapers were intemperate in their criticism of the government, and a campaign was carried on openly which aimed at changing from a monarchy to a democracy, without any apparent molestation from the authorities. All these things impressed the lad who had seen in his own country the most respectfully worded complaints of unquestionable abuses treated as treason, bringing not merely punishment, but opprobrium as well.

He, himself, in order to obtain a better education, had had to leave his country stealthily like a fugitive from justice, and his family, to save themselves from persecution, were compelled to profess ignorance of his plans and movements. His name was entered in Santo Tomás at the opening of the new term, with the fees paid, and Paciano had gone to Manila pretending to be looking for this brother whom he had assisted out of the country.

Early in the fall Rizal removed to Madrid and entered the Central University there. His short residence in Barcelona was possibly for the purpose of correcting the irregularity in his passport, for in that town it would be easier to obtain a cedula, and with this his way in the national University would be made smoother. He enrolled in two courses, medicine, and literature and philosophy; besides these he studied sculpture, drawing and art in San Carlos, and took private lessons in languages from Mr. Hughes, a well-known instructor of the city. With all these labors it is not strange that he did not mingle largely in social life, and lack of funds and want of clothes, which have been suggested as reasons for this, seem hardly adequate. José had left Manila with some seven hundred pesos and a diamond ring. Besides, he received funds from his father monthly, which were sent through his cousin, Antonio Rivera, of Manila, for fear that the landlords might revenge themselves upon their tenant for the slight which his son had cast upon their university in deserting it for a Peninsular institution. It was no easy task in those days for a lad from the provinces to get out of the Islands for study abroad.

Rizal frequently attended the theater, choosing especially the higher class dramas, occasionally went to a masked ball, played the lotteries in small amounts but regularly, and for the rest devoted most of his money to the purchase of books. The greater part of these were second-hand, but he bought several standard works in good editions, many with bindings de luxe. Among the books first purchased figure a Spanish translation of the "Lives of the Presidents of the United States," from Washington to Johnson, morocco bound, gilt-edged, and illustrated with steel engravings—certainly an expensive book; a "History of the English Revolution;" a comparison of the Romans and the Teutons, and several other books which indicated interest in the freer system of the AngloSaxons. Later, another "History of the Presidents," to Cleveland, was added to his library.

The following lines, said to be addressed to his mother, were written about this time, evidently during an attack of homesickness:

"You Ask Me for Verses"

(Translated by Charles Derbyshire)

You bid me now to strike the lyre,
That mute and torn so long has lain; And yet I cannot wake the strain,
Nor will the Muse one note inspire!
Coldly it shakes in accents dire,
As if my soul itself to wring,
And when its sound seems but to fling
A jest at its own low lament;

So in sad isolation pent,
My soul can neither feel nor sing.

There was a time—ah, 'tis too true—
But that time long ago has past— When upon me the Muse had cast
Indulgent smile and friendship's due;

But of that age now all too few
The thoughts that with me yet will stay;
As from the hours of festive play
There linger on mysterious notes,

And in our minds the memory floats   Of minstrelsy and music gay.

A plant I am, that scarcely grown,
Was torn from out its Eastern bed,
Where all around perfume is shed,
And life but as a dream is known;   The land that I can call my own,

By me forgotten ne'er to be,
Where trilling birds their song taught me,
And cascades with their ceaseless roar,   And all along the spreading shore   The murmurs of the sounding sea.

While yet in childhood's happy day,
I learned upon its sun to smile,
And in my breast there seemed the while   Seething volcanic fires to play.
A bard I was, and my wish alway   To call upon the fleeting wind,
With all the force of verse and mind:
"Go forth, and spread around its fame,
From zone to zone with glad acclaim,
And earth to heaven together bind!"

But it I left, and now no more—   Like a tree that is broken and sere—
My natal gods bring the echo clear
Of songs that in past times they bore;
Wide seas I cross'd to foreign shore,
With hope of change and other fate;
My folly was made clear too late,

For in the place of good I sought The seas reveal'd unto me naught, But made death's specter on me wait.

All these fond fancies that were mine,
All love, all feeling, all emprise,
Were left beneath the sunny skies,
Which o'er that flowery region shine; So press no more that plea of thine,

For songs of love from out a heart
That coldly lies a thing apart;
Since now with tortur'd soul I haste Unresting o'er the desert waste, And lifeless gone is all my art.

In Madrid a number of young Filipinos were intense enthusiasts over political agitation, and with the recklessness of youth, were careless of what they said or how they said it, so long as it brought no danger to them. A sort of Philippine social club had been organized by older Filipinos and Spaniards interested in the Philippines, with the idea of quietly assisting toward improved insular conditions, but it became so radical under the influence of this younger majority, that its conservative members were compelled to drop out and the club broke up. The young men were constantly holding meetings to revive it, but never arrived at any effective conclusions. Rizal was present at some of these meetings and suggested that a good means of propaganda would be a book telling the truth about Philippine conditions and illustrated by Filipino artists. At first the project was severely criticised; later a few conformed to the plan, and Rizal believed that his scheme was in a fair way of accomplishment. At the meeting to discuss the details, however, each member of the company wanted to write upon the Filipino woman, and therest of the subjects scarcely interested any of them. Rizal was disgusted with this trifling and dropped the affair, nor did he ever again seem to take any very enthusiastic interest in such popular movements. His more mature mind put him out of sympathy with the younger men.

Their admiration gave him great prestige, but his popularity did not arise from comradeship, as he had but very few intimates.

Early in his stay in Madrid, Rizal had come across a second-hand copy, in two volumes, of a French novel, which he bought to improve his knowledge of that language. It was Eugene Sue's "The Wandering Jew," that work which transformed the France of the nineteenth century. However one may agree or disagree with its teachings and concede or dispute its literary merits, it cannot be denied that it was the most powerful book in its effects on the century, surpassing even Mrs. Stowe's "Uncle Tom's Cabin," which is usually credited with having hurried on the American Civil War and brought about the termination of African slavery in the United States. The book, he writes in his diary, affected him powerfully, not to tears, but with a tremendous sympathy for the unfortunates that made him willing to risk everything in their behalf. It seemed to him that such a presentation of Philippine conditions would certainly arouse Spain, but his modesty forbade his saying that he was going to write a book like the French masterpiece. Still, from this time his recollections of his youth and the stories which he could get from his companions were written down and revised, till finally the half had been prepared of what was finally the novel "Noli Me Tangere."

Through Spaniards who still remembered José's uncle, he joined a lodge of Masons called the "Acacia." At this time few Filipinos in Spain had joined the institution, and those were mostly men much more mature than himself. Thus he met leaders of Spanish national life who were men of state affairs and much more sedate, men with broader views and more settled opinions than the irresponsible class with whom his school companions were accustomed to associate. A distinction must be made between the Masonry of this time and the much more popular institution in which Filipinos later figured so largely when Professor Miguel Morayta became head of the Grand Lodge which for a time was a rival of that to which the "Acacia" owed allegiance, and finally triumphed over it.

In 1884 Rizal had begun his studies in English; he had been studying French during and since his voyage to Spain; Italian was acquired apparently at a time when the exposition of Genoa had attracted Spanish interest toward Italy, and largely through the reading of Italian translations of works which he knew in other languages. German, too, he had started to study, but had not advanced far with it. Thus Rizal was preparing himself for the travels through Europe which he had intended to make from the time when he first left his home, for he well knew that it was only by knowing the language of a country that it would be possible for him to study the people, see in what way they differed from his own, and find out which of their customs and what lessons from their history might be of advantage to the Filipinos.

A feature in Rizal's social life was a weekly visit to the home of Don Pablo Ortigas y Reyes, a liberal Spaniard who had been Civil Governor of Manila in General de La Torre's time. Here Filipino students gathered, and were entertained by the charming daughter of the home, Consuelo, who was the person to whom were dedicated the verses of Rizal usually entitled "á la Senorita C. O. y R."

In Rizal's later days he found a regular relaxation in playing chess, in which he was skilled, with the venerable ex-president of the short-lived Spanish republic, Pi y Margal. This statesman was accused of German tendencies because of his inclination toward Anglo-Saxon safeguards for liberty, and was a champion of general education as a preparation for a freer Spain.

Rizal usually was present on public occasions in Filipino circles and took a leading part in them, as, for example, when he delivered the principal address at the banquet given by the Madrid Filipino colony in honor of their artist countrymen, after Luna and Hidalgo had won prizes in the Madrid National exposition. He was also at the New Year's banquet when the students gathered in the restaurant to bid farewell to the old and usher in the new year, and his was the chief speech, summarizing the remarks of the others.

In 1885, having completed the second of his two courses, with his credentials of licentiate in medicine and also in philosophy and literature, Rizal made a trip through the country provinces to study the Spanish peasant, for the rural people, he thought, being agriculturists, would be most like the farmer folk of his native land. Surely the Filipinos did not suffer in the comparison, for the Spanish peasants had not greatly changed from the day when they were so masterfully described by Cervantes. It seemed to Rizal almost like being in Don Quixote's land, so many were the figures who might have been the characters in the book.

The fall of '85 found Rizal in Paris, studying art, visiting the various museums and associating with the Lunas, the Taveras and other Filipino residents of the French capital, for there had been a considerable colony in that city ever since the troubles of 1872 had driven the Tavera family into exile and they had made their home in that city. In Paris a fourth of "Noli Me Tangere" was written, and Rizal specialized in ophthalmology, devoting his attention to those eye troubles that were most prevalent in the Philippines and least understood. His mother's growing blindness made him covet the skill which might enable him to restore her sight. So successfully did he study that he became the favorite pupil of Doctor L. de Weckert, the leading authority among the oculists of France, and author of a three-volume standard work. Rizal next went to Germany, having continued his studies in its language in the French capital, and was present at Heidelberg on the five hundredth anniversary of the foundation of the University.

Because he had no passport he could only attend lectures, but could not regularly matriculate. He lived in one of the student boarding houses, with a number of law students, and when he was proposed for membership in the Chess Club he was registered in the Club books as being a student of law like the men who proposed him. These Chess Club gatherings were quite a feature of the town, being held in the large saloons with several hundred people present, and the contests of skill were eagerly watched by shrewd and competent judges. Rizal was a clever player, and left something of a record among the experts.

The following lines were written by Rizal in a letter home while he was a student in Germany:

To the Flowers of Heidelberg

(translation by Charles Derbyshire)

Go to my native land, go, foreign flowers,
Sown by the traveler on his way;
And there beneath its azure sky,
Where all of my affections lie;
There from the weary pilgrim say,

What faith is his in that land of ours!

Go there and tell how when the dawn,
Her early light diffusing,
Your petals first flung open wide;
His steps beside chill Neckar drawn, You see him silent by your side, Upon its Spring perennial musing.

Saw how when morning's light,
All your fragrance stealing,
Whispers to you as in mirth
Playful songs of love's delight,
He, too, murmurs his love's feeling In the tongue he learned at birth.

That when the sun on Koenigstuhl's height
Pours out its golden flood,

And with its slowly warming light
Gives life vale and grove and wood,
He greets that sun, here only upraising, Which in his native land is at its zenith blazing.

And tell there of that day he stood,
Near to a ruin'd castle gray,

By Neckar's banks, or shady wood,
And pluck'd you from beside the way;
Tell, too, the tale to you addressed,
And how with tender care,
Your bending leaves he press'd 'Twixt pages of some volume rare.

Bear then, O flowers, love's message bear;
My love to all the lov'd ones there,
Peace to my country—fruitful land—
Faith whereon its sons may stand,
And virtue for its daughters' care;
All those belovéd creatures greet, That still around home's altar meet.

And when you come unto its shore,
This kiss I now on you bestow,
Fling where the winged breezes blow; That borne on them it may hover o'er All that I love, esteem, and adore.

But though, O flowers, you come unto that land,
And still perchance your colors hold;
So far from this heroic strand,
Whose soil first bade your life unfold,

Still here your fragrance will expand; Your soul that never quits the earth Whose light smiled on you at your birth.

From Heidelberg he went to Leipzig, then famous for the new studies in psychology which were making the science of the mind almost as exact as that of the body, and became interested in the comparison of race characteristics as influenced by environment, history and language. This probably accounts for the advanced views held by Rizal, who was thoroughly abreast of the new psychology. These ideas were since popularized in America largely through Professor Hugo Munsterberg of Harvard University, who was a fellow-student of Rizal at Heidelberg and also had been at Leipzig.

A little later Rizal went to Berlin and there became acquainted with a number of men who had studied the Philippines and knew it as none whom he had ever met previously. Chief among these was Doctor Jagor, the author of the book which ten years before had inspired in him his life purpose of preparing his people for the time when America should come to the Philippines. Then there was Doctor Rudolf Virchow, head of the Anthropological Society and one of the greatest scientists in the world. Virchow was of intensely democratic ideals, he was a statesman as well as a scientist, and the interest of the young student in the history of his country and in everything else which concerned it, and his sincere earnestness, so intelligently directed toward helping his country, made Rizal at once a prime favorite. Under Virchow's sponsorship he became a member of the Berlin Anthropological Society.

Rizal lived in the third floor of a corner lodging house not very far from the University; in this room he spent much of his time, putting the finishing touches to what he had previously written of his novel, and there he wrote the latter half of "Noli Me Tangere" The German influence, and absence from the Philippines for so long a time, had modified his early radical views, and the book had now become less an effort to arouse the Spanish sense of justice than a means of education for Filipinos by pointing out their shortcomings. Perhaps a Spanish school history which he had read in Madrid deserves a part of the credit for this changed point of view, since in that the author, treating of Spain's early misfortunes, brings out the fact that misgovernment may be due quite as much to the hypocrisy, servility and undeserving character of the people as it is to the corruption, tyranny and cruelty of the rulers.

The printer of "Noli Me Tangere" lived in a neighboring street, and, like most printers in Germany, worked for a very moderate compensation, so that the volume of over four hundred pages cost less than a fourth of what it would have done in England, or one half of what it would cost in economical Spain. Yet even at so modest a price, Rizal was delayed in the publication until one fortunate morning he received a visit from a countryman, Doctor Maximo Viola, who invited him to take a pedestrian trip. Rizal responded that his interests kept him in Berlin at that time as he was awaiting funds from home with which to publish a book he had just completed, and showed him the manuscript. Doctor Viola was much interested and offered to use the money he had put aside for the trip to help pay the publisher. So the work went ahead, and when the delayed remittance from his family arrived, Rizal repaid the obligation. Then the two sallied forth on their trip.

After a considerable tour of the historic spots and scenic places in Germany, they arrived at Dresden, where Doctor Rizal was warmly greeted by Doctor A. B. Meyer, the Director of the Royal Saxony Ethnographical Institute. He was an authority upon Philippine matters, for some years before he had visited the Islands to make a study of the people. With a countryman resident in the Philippines, Doctor Meyer made careful and thorough scientific investigations, and his conclusions were more favorable to the Filipinos than the published views of many of the unscientific Spanish observers.

In the Museum of Art at Dresden, Rizal saw a painting of "Prometheus Bound," which recalled to him a representation of the same idea in a French gallery, and from memory he modeled this figure, which especially appealed to him as being typical of his country.

In Austrian territory he first visited Doctor Ferdinand Blumentritt, whom Rizal had known by reputation for many years and with whom he had long corresponded. The two friends stayed at the Hotel Roderkrebs, but were guests at the table of the Austrian professor, whose wife gave them appetizing demonstrations of the characteristic cookery of Hungary. During Rizal's stay he was very much interested in a gathering of tourists, arranged to make known the beauties of that picturesque region, sometimes called the Austrian Switzerland, and he delivered an address upon this occasion. It is noteworthy that the present interest in attracting tourists to the Philippines, as an economic benefit to the country, was anticipated by Doctor Rizal and that he was always looking up methods used in foreign countries for building up tourists' travel.

One day, while the visitors were discussing
Philippine matters with their host, Doctor
Rizal made an off hand sketch of Doctor Blumentritt, on a scrap of paper which happened to be at hand, so characteristic that it serves as an excellent portrait, and it has been preserved among the Rizal relics which Doctor Blumentritt had treasured of the friend for whom he had so much respect and affection.

With a letter of introduction to a friend of Doctor Blumentritt in Vienna, Nordenfels, the greatest of Austrian novelists, Doctor Viola and Doctor Rizal went on to the capital, where they were entertained by the Concordia Club. So favorable was the impression that Rizal made upon Mr. Nordenfels that an answer was written to the note of introduction, thanking the professor for having brought to his notice a person whom he had found so companionable and whose genius he so much admired. Nordenfels had been interested in Spanish subjects, and was able to discuss intelligently the peculiar development of Castilian civilization and the politics of the Spanish metropolis as they affected the overseas possessions.

After having seen Rome and a little more of Italy, they embarked for the Philippines, again on the French mail, from Marseilles, coming by way of Saigon, where a rice steamer was taken for Manila.

CHAPTER VII

The Period of Propaganda

The city had not altered much during Rizal's seven years of absence. The condition of the Binondo pavement, with the same holes in the road which Rizal claimed he remembered as a schoolboy, was unchanged, and this recalls the experience of Ybarra in "Noli Me Tangere" on his homecoming after a like period of absence.

Doctor Rizal at once went to his home in
Kalamba. His first operation in the Philippines relieved the blindness of his mother, by the removal of a double cataract, and thus the object of his special study in Paris was accomplished. This and other like successes gave the young oculist a fame which brought patients from all parts of Luzon; and, though his charges were moderate, during his seven months' stay in the Islands Doctor Rizal accumulated over five thousand pesos, besides a number of diamonds which he had bought as a secure way of carrying funds, mindful of the help that the ring had been with which he had first started from the Philippines.

Shortly after his arrival, Governor-General
Terrero summoned Rizal by telegraph to Malacañan from Kalamba. The interview proved to be due to the interest in the author of "Noli Me Tangere" and a curiosity to read the novel, arising from the copious extracts with which the Manila censors had submitted an unfavorable opinion when asking for the prohibition of the book. The recommendation of the censor was disregarded, and General Terrero, fearful that Rizal might be molested by some of the many persons who would feel themselves aggrieved by his plain picturing of undesirable classes in the Philippines, gave him for a bodyguard a young Spanish lieutenant, José Taviel de Andrade. The young men soon became fast friends, as they had artistic and other tastes in common. Once they climbed Mr. Makiling, near Kalamba, and placed there, after the European custom, a flag to show that they had reached the summit. This act was at first misrepresented by the enemies of Rizal as planting a German banner, for they started a story that he had taken possession of the Islands in the name of the country where he was educated, which was just then in unfriendly relations with Spain over the question of the ill treatment of the Protestant missionaries in the Caroline Islands. This same story was repeated after the American occupation with the variation that Rizal, as the supreme chief and originator of the ideas of

the Katipunan (which in fact he was not—he was even opposed to the society as it existed in his time), had placed there a Filipino banner, in token that the Islands intended to reassume the independent condition of which the Spanish had dispossessed them.

"Noli Me Tangere" circulated first among Doctor Rizal's relatives; on one occasion a cousin made a special trip to Kalamba and took the author to task for having caricatured her in the character of Doña Victorina. Rizal made no denial, but merely suggested that the book was a mirror of Philippine life, with types that unquestionably existed in the country, and that if anybody recognized one of the characters as picturing himself or herself, that person would do well to correct the faults which therein appeared ridiculous.

A somewhat liberal administration was now governing the Philippines, and efforts were being made to correct the more glaring abuses in the social conditions. One of these reforms proposed that the larger estates should bear their share of the taxes, which it was believed they were then escaping to a great extent. Requests were made of the municipal government of Kalamba, among other towns, for a statement of the relation that the big Dominican hacienda bore to the town, what increase or decrease there might have been in the income of the estate, and what taxes the proprietors were paying compared with the revenue their place afforded.

Rizal interested the people of the community to gather reliable statistics, to go thoroughly into the actual conditions, and to leave out the generalities which usually characterized Spanish documents.

He asked the people to coöperate, pointing out that when they did not complain it was their own fault more than that of the government if they suffered injustice. Further, he showed the folly of exaggerated statements, and insisted upon a definite and moderate showing of such abuses as were unquestionably within the power of the authorities to relieve. Rizal himself prepared the report, which is an excellent presentation of the grievances of the people of his town. It brings forward as special points in favor of the community their industriousness, their willingness to help themselves, their interest in education, and concludes with expressing confidence in the fairness of the government, pointing out the fact that they were risking the displeasure of their landlords by furnishing the information requested. The paper made a big stir, and its essential statements, like everything else in Rizal's writings, were never successfully challenged.

Conditions in Manila were at that time disturbed owing to the precedence which had been given in a local festival to the Chinese, because they paid more money. The Filipinos claimed that, being in their home country, they should have had prior consideration and were entitled to it by law. The matter culminated in a protest, which was doubtless submitted to Doctor Rizal on the eve of his departure from the Islands; the protest in a general way met with his approval, but the theatrical methods adopted in the presentation of it can hardly have been according to his advice.

He sailed for Hongkong in February of 1888, and made a short stay in the British colony, becoming acquainted there with Jose Maria Basa, an exile of '72, who had constituted himself the especial guardian of the Filipino students in that city. The visitor was favorably impressed by the methods of education in the British colony and with the spirit of patriotism developed thereby. He also looked into the subject of the large investments in Hongkong property by the corporation landlords of the Philippines, their preparation for the day of trouble which they foresaw.

Rizal was interested in the Chinese theater, comparing the plays with the somewhat similar productions which existed in the Philippines; there, however, they had been given a religious twist, which at first glance hid their debt to the Chinese drama. The Doctor notes meeting, at nearby Macao, an exile of '72, whose condition and patient, uncomplaining bearing of his many troubles aroused Rizal's sympathies and commanded his admiration.

With little delay, the journey was continued to Japan, where Doctor Rizal was surprised by an invitation to make his home in the Spanish consulate. There he was hospitably entertained, and a like courtesy was shown him in the Spanish minister's home in Tokio. The latter even offered him a position, as a sort of interpreter, probably, should he care to remain in the country. This offer, however, was declined. Rizal made considerable investigation into the condition of the various Japanese classes and acquired such facility in the use of the language that with it and his appearance, for he was "very Japanese," the natives found it difficult to believe that he was not one of themselves. The month or more passed here he considered one of the happiest in his travels, and it was with regret that he sailed from Yokohama for San Francisco. A Japanese newspaper man, who knew no other language than his own, was a companion on the entire journey to London, and Rizal acted as his interpreter.

Not only did he enter into the spirit of the language but with remarkable versatility he absorbed the spirit of the Japanese artists and acquired much dexterity in expressing himself in their style, as is shown by one of the illustrations in this book. The popular idea that things occidental are reversed in the Orient was amusingly caricatured in a sketch he made of a German face; by reversing its lines he converted it into an old-time Japanese countenance.

The diary of the voyage from Hongkong to Japan records an incident to which he alludes as being similar to that of Aladdin in the Tagalog tale of Florante. The Filipino wife of an Englishman, Mrs. Jackson, who was a passenger on board, told Rizal a great deal about a Filipino named Rachal, who was educated in Europe and had written a muchtalked-of novel, which she described and of which she spoke in such flattering terms that Rizal declared his identity. The confusion in names is explained by the fact that Rachal is a name well known in the Philippines as that of a popular make of piano.

At San Francisco the boat was held for some time in quarantine because of sickness aboard, and Rizal was impressed by the fact that the valuable cargo of silk was not delayed but was quickly transferred to the shore. His diary is illustrated with a drawing of the Treasury flag on the customs launch which acted as go-between for their boat and the shore. Finally, the first-class passengers were allowed to land, and he went to the Palace Hotel.

With little delay, the overland journey was begun; the scenery through the picturesque Rocky Mountains especially impressed him, and finally Chicago was reached. The thing that struck him most forcibly in that city was the large number of cigar stores with an Indian in front of each—and apparently no two Indians alike. The unexpressed idea was that in America the remembrance of the first inhabitants of the land and their dress was retained and popularized, while in the Philippines knowledge of the first inhabitants of the land was to be had only from foreign museums.

Niagara Falls is the next impression recorded in the diary, which has been preserved and is now in the Newberry Library of Chicago. The same strange, awe-inspiring mystery which others have found in the big falls affected him, but characteristically he compared this world-wonder with the cascades of his native La Laguna, claiming for them greater delicacy and a daintier enchantment.

From Albany, the train ran along the banks of the Hudson, and he was reminded of the Pasig in his homeland, with its much greater commerce and its constant activity.

At New York, Rizal embarked on the City of Rome, then the finest steamer in the world, and after a pleasant voyage, in which his spare moments were occupied in rereading
"Gulliver's Travels" in English, Rizal reached England, and said good-by to the friends whom he had met during their brief ocean trip together.

Rizal's first letters home to his family speak of being in the free air of England and once more amidst European activity. For a short time he lived with Doctor Antonio Maria Regidor, an exile of '72, who had come to secure what Spanish legal Business he could in the British metropolis. Doctor Regidor was formerly an official in the Philippines, and later proved his innocence of any complicity in the troubles of '72.

Doctor Rizal then boarded with a Mr.
Beckett, organist of St. Paul's Church, at 37
Charlecote Crescent, in the favorite North West residence section. The zoölogical gardens were conveniently near and the British Museum was within easy walking distance. The new member was a favorite with all the family, which consisted of three daughters besides the father and mother.

Rizal's youthful interest in sleight-of-hand tricks was still maintained. During his stay in the Philippines he had sometimes amused his friends in this way, till one day he was horrified to find that the simple country folk, who were also looking on, thought that he was working miracles. In London he resumed his favorite diversion, and a Christmas gift of
Mrs. Beckett to him, "The Life and
Adventures of Valentine Vox the
Ventriloquist," indicated the interest his friends took in this amusement. One of his own purchases was "Modern Magic," the frontispiece of which is the sphinx that figures in the story of "El Filibusterismo."

It was Rizal's custom to study the deceptions practiced upon the peoples of other lands, comparing them with those of which his own countrymen had been victims. Thus he could get an idea of the relative credulity of different peoples and could also account for many practices the origin of which was otherwise less easy to understand. His investigations were both in books and by personal research. In quest of these experiences he one day chanced to visit a professional phrenologist; the bump-reader was a shrewd guesser, for he dwelt especially upon Rizal's aptitude for learning languages and advised him to take up the study of them.

This interest in languages, shown in his childish ambition to be like Sir John Bowring, made Rizal a congenial companion of a still more distinguished linguist, Doctor Reinhold Rost, the librarian of the India

Office. The Raffles Library in Singapore now owns Doctor Rost's library, and its collection of grammars in seventy languages attests the wide range of the studies of this Sanscrit scholar.

Doctor Rost was born and educated in Germany, though naturalized as a British subject, and he was a man of great musical taste. His family sometimes formed an orchestra, at other times a glee club, and furnished all the necessary parts from its own members. Rizal was a frequent visitor, usually spending his Sundays in athletic exercises with the boys, for he quickly became proficient in the English sports of boxing and cricket. While resting he would converse with the father, or chat with the daughters of the home. All the children had literary tastes, and one, Daisy, presented him with a copy of a novel which she had just translated from the German, entitled "Ulli." Some idea of Doctor Rizal's own linguistic attainments may be gained from the fact that instead of writing letters to his nephews and nieces he made for them translations of some of Hans Christian Andersen's fairy tales. They consist of some forty manuscript pages, profusely illustrated, and the father is referred to in a "dedication," as though it were a real book. The Hebrew Bible quotation is in allusion to a jocose remark once made by the father that German was like Hebrew to him, the verse being that in which the sons of Jacob, not recognizing that their brother was the seller, were bargaining for some of Pharaoh's surplus corn, "And he (Joseph) said, How is the old man, your father?" Rizal always tried to relieve by a touch of humor anything that seemed to him as savoring of affectation, the phase of Spanish character that repelled him and the imitation of which by his countrymen who knew nothing of the un-Spanish world disgusted him with them.

Another example of his versatility in language and of its usefulness to him as well, is shown in a trilingual letter written by Rizal in Dapitan when the censorship of his correspondence had become annoying through ignorant exceptions to perfectly harmless matters. No Spaniard available spoke more than one language besides his own and it was necessary to send the letter to three different persons to find out its contents. The critics took the hint and Rizal received better treatment thereafter.

Another one of Rizal's youthful aspirations was attained in London, for there he began transcribing the early Spanish history by Morga of which Sir John Bowring had told his uncle. A copy of this rare book was in the British Museum and he gained admission as a reader there through the recommendation of Doctor Rost. Only five hundred persons can be accommodated in the big reading room, and as students are coming from every continent for special researches, good reason has to be shown why these studies cannot be made at some other institution.

Besides the copying of the text of Morga's history, Rizal read many other early writings on the Philippines, and the manifest unfairness of some of these who thought that they could glorify Spain only by disparaging the Filipinos aroused his wrath. Few Spanish writers held up the good name of those who were under their flag, and Rizal had to resort to foreign authorities to disprove their libels. Morga was almost alone among Spanish historians, but his assertions found corroboration in the contemporary chronicles of other nationalities. Rizal spent his evenings in the home of Doctor Regidor, and many a time the bitterness and impatience with which his day's work in the Museum had inspired him, would be forgotten as the older man counseled patience and urged that such prejudices were to be expected of a little educated nation. Then Rizal's brow would clear as he quoted his favorite proverb, "To understand all is to forgive all."

Doctor Rost was editor of Trübner's Record, a journal devoted to the literature of the East, founded by the famous Oriental Bookseller and Publisher of London, Nicholas Trübner, and Doctor Rizal contributed to it in May, 1889, some specimens of Tagal folklore, an extract from which is appended, as it was then printed:

Specimens of Tagal Folklore

By Doctor J. Rizal

Proverbial Sayings

Malakas ang bulong sa sigaw, Low words are stronger than loud words.

Ang lakí sa layaw karaniwa 'y hubad, A petted child is generally naked (i.e. poor).

Hampasng magulang ay nakatabã, Parents' punishment makes one fat.

Ibang hari ibang ugail, New king, new fashion.

Nagpupútol ang kapus, ang labis ay nagdurugtong, What is short cuts off a piece from itself, what is long adds another on (the poor gets poorer, the rich richer).

Ang nagsasabing tapus ay siyang kinakapus, He who finishes his words finds himself wanting.

Nangangakõ habang napapakõ, Man promises while in need.

Ang naglalakad ng maráhan, matinik may mababaw, He who walks slowly, though he may put his foot on a thorn, will not be hurt very much (Tagals mostly go barefooted).

Ang maniwalã sa sabi 'y walang bait na sarili, He who believes in tales has no own mind.

Ang may isinuksok sa dingding, ay may titingalain, He who has put something between the wall may afterwards look on (the saving man may afterwards be cheerful).— The wall of a Tagal house is made of palmleaves and bamboo, so that it can be used as a cupboard.

Walang mahirap gisingin na paris nang nagtutulogtulugan, The most difficult to rouse from sleep is the man who pretends to be asleep.

Labis sa salitã, kapus sa gawã, Too many words, too little work.

Hipong tulog ay nadadalá ng ánod, The sleeping shrimp is carried away by the current.

Sa bibig nahuhuli ang isda, The fish is caught through the mouth.

Puzzles

Isang butil na palay sikip sa buony bahay, One rice-corn fills up all the house.—The light. The rice-corn with the husk is yellowish.

Matapang akó so dalawá, duag akó sa isá, I am brave against two, coward against one.— The bamboo bridge. When the bridge is made of one bamboo only, it is difficult to pass over; but when it is made of two or more, it is very easy.

Dalá akó niya, dalá ko siya, He carries me, I carry him.—The shoes.

Isang balong malalim puna ng patalím, A deep well filled with steel blades.—The mouth.

The Filipino colony in Spain had established a fortnightly review, published first in Barcelona and later in Madrid, to enlighten Spaniards on their distant colony, and Rizal wrote for it from the start. Its name, La Solidaridad, perhaps may be translated Equal Rights, as it aimed at like laws and the same privileges for the Peninsula and the possessions overseas.

From the Philippines came news of a contemptible attempt to reach Rizal through his family—one of many similar petty persecutions. His sister Lucia's husband had died and the corpse was refused interment in consecrated ground, upon the pretext that the dead man, who had been exceptionally liberal to the church and was of unimpeachable character, had been negligent in his religious duties. Another individual with a notorious record of longer absence from confession died about the same time, and his funeral took place from the church without demur. The ugly feature about the refusal to bury Hervosa was that the telegram from the friar parish-priest to the Archbishop at Manila in asking instructions, was careful to mention that the deceased was a brother-in-law of Rizal. Doctor Rizal wrote a scorching article for La Solidaridad under the caption "An Outrage," and took the matter up with the Spanish Colonial Minister, then Becerra, a professed Liberal. But that weakling statesman, more liberal in words than in actions, did nothing.

That the union of Church and State can be as demoralizing to religion as it is disastrous to good government seems sufficiently established by Philippine incidents like this, in which politics was substituted for piety as the test of a good Catholic, making marriage impossible and denying decent burial to the families of those who differed politically with the ministers of the national religion.

Of all his writings, the article in which Rizal speaks of this indignity to the dead comes nearest to exhibiting personal feeling and rancor. Yet his main point is to indicate generally what monstrous conditions the Philippine mixture of religion and politics made possible.

The following are part of a series of nineteen verses published in La Solidaridad over Rizal's favorite pen name of Laong Laan:

To my Muse

(translation by Charles Derbyshire)

Invoked no longer is the Muse,

The lyre is out of date;
The poets it no longer use,
And youth its inspiration now imbues With other form and state.

If today our fancies aught
Of verse would still require,

Helicon's hill remains unsought;
And without heed we but inquire,   Why the coffee is not brought.

In the place of thought sincere
That our hearts may feel,
We must seize a pen of steel,
And with verse and line severe   Fling abroad a jest and jeer.

Muse, that in the past inspired me,
And with songs of love hast fired me;
Go thou now to dull repose,   For today in sordid prose
I must earn the gold that hired me.

Now must I ponder deep,
Meditate, and struggle on;
E'en sometimes I must weep;   For he who love would keep
Great pain has undergone.

Fled are the days of ease,
The days of Love's delight;

When flowers still would please
And give to suffering souls surcease   From pain and sorrow's blight.

One by one they have passed on,
All I loved and moved among;
Dead or married—from me gone,   For all I place my heart
upon   By fate adverse are stung.   Go thou, too, O Muse,
depart,

Other regions fairer find;
For my land but offers art
For the laurel, chains that bind,   For a temple, prisons blind.

But before thou leavest me, speak:

Tell me with thy voice sublime,
Thou couldst ever from me seek A song of sorrow for the weak, Defiance to the tyrant's crime.

Rizal's congenial situation in the British capital was disturbed by his discovering a growing interest in the youngest of the three girls whom he daily met. He felt that his career did not permit him to marry, nor was his youthful affection for his cousin in Manila an entirely forgotten sentiment. Besides, though he never lapsed into such disregard for his feminine friends as the low Spanish standard had made too common among the
Filipino students in Madrid, Rizal was ever on his guard against himself. So he suggested to Doctor Regidor that he considered it would be better for him to leave London. His parting gift to the family with whom he had lived so happily was a clay medallion bearing in relief the profiles of the three sisters.

Other regretful good-bys were said to a number of young Filipinos whom he had gathered around him and formed into a club for the study of the history of their country and the discussion of its politics.

Rizal now went to Paris, where he was glad to be again with his friend Valentin Ventura, a wealthy Pampangan who had been trained for the law. His tastes and ideals were very much those of Rizal, and he had sound sense and a freedom from affectation which especially appealed to Rizal. There Rizal's reprint of Morga's rare history was made, at a greater cost but also in better form than his first novel. Copious notes gave references to other authorities and compared present with past conditions, and Doctor Blumentritt contributed a forceful introduction.

When Rizal returned to London to correct the proofsheets, the old original book was in use and the copy could not be checked. This led to a number of errors, misspelled and changed words, and even omissions of sentences, which were afterwards discovered and carefully listed and filed away to be corrected in another edition.

Possibly it has been made clear already that, while Rizal did not work for separation from Spain, he was no admirer of the Castilian character, nor of the Latin type, for that matter. He remarked on Blumentritt's comparison of the Spanish rulers in the Philippines with the Czars of Russia, that it is flattering to the Castilians but it is more than they merit, to put them in the same class as Russia. Apparently he had in mind the somewhat similar comparison in Burke's speech on the conciliation of America, in which he said that Russia was more advanced and less cruel than Spain and so not to be classed with it.

During his stay in Paris, Rizal was a frequent visitor at the home of the two Doctors Pardo de Tavera, sons of the exile of '72 who had gone to France, the younger now a physician in South America, the elder a former Philippine Commissioner. The interest of the one in art, and of the other in philology, the ideas of progress through education shared by both, and many other common tastes and ideals, made the two young men fast friends of Rizal. Mrs. Tavera, the mother, was an interesting conversationalist, and Rizal profited by her reminiscences of Philippine official life, to the inner circle of which her husband's position had given her the entrée.

On Sundays Rizal fenced at Juan Luna's house with his distinguished artistcountryman, or, while the latter was engaged with Ventura, watched their play. It was on one of these afternoons that the Tagalog story of "The Monkey and the Tortoise"[2] was hastily sketched as a joke to fill the remaining pages of Mrs. Luna's autograph album, in which she had been insisting Rizal must write before all its space was used up. A comparison of the Tagalog version with a Japanese counterpart was published by Rizal in English, in Trübner's Magazine, suggesting that the two people may have had a common origin. This study received considerable attention from other ethnologists, and was among the topics at an ethnological conference.

At times his antagonist was Miss Nellie Baustead, who had great skill with the foils. Her father, himself born in the Philippines, the son of a wealthy merchant of Singapore, had married a member of the Genato family of Manila. At their villa in Biarritz, and again in their home in Belgium, Rizal was a guest later, for Mr. Baustead had taken a great liking to him.

The teaching instinct that led him to act as mentor to the Filipino students in Spain and made him the inspiration of a mutual improvement club of his young countrymen in London, suggested the foundation of a school in Paris. Later a Pampangan youth offered him $40,000 with which to found a Filipino college in Hongkong, where many young men from the Philippines had obtained an education better than their own land could afford but not entirely adapted to their needs. The scheme attracted Rizal, and a prospectus for such an institution which was later found among his papers not only proves how deeply he was interested, but reveals the fact that his ideas of education were essentially like those carried out in the present public-school course of instruction in the Philippines.

Early in August of 1890 Rizal went to Madrid to seek redress for a wrong done his family by the notorious General Weyler, the "Butcher" of evil memory in Cuba, then Governor-General of the Philippines. Just as the mother's loss of liberty, years before, was caused by revengeful feelings on the part of an official because for one day she was obliged to omit a customary gift of horse feed, so the father's loss of land was caused by a revengeful official, and for quite as trivial a cause.

Mr. Mercado was a great poultry fancier and especially prided himself upon his fine stock of turkeys. He had been accustomed to respond to the frequent requests of the estate agent for presents of birds. But at one time disease had so reduced the number of turkeys that all that remained were needed for breeding purposes and Mercado was obliged to refuse him. In a rage the agent insisted, and when that proved unavailing, threats followed.

But Francisco Mercado was not a man to be moved by threats, and when the next rent day came round he was notified that his rent had been doubled. This was paid without protest, for the tenants were entirely at the mercy of the landlords, no fixed rate appearing either in contracts or receipts. Then the rent-raising was kept on till Mercado was driven to seek the protection of the courts. Part of his case led to exactly the same situation as that of the Biñan tenantry in his grandfather's time, when the landlords were compelled to produce their title-deeds, and these proved that land of others had been illegally included in the estate. Other tenants, emboldened by Mercado's example also refused to pay the exorbitant rent increases.

The justice of the peace of Kalamba, before whom the case first came, was threatened by the provincial governor for taking time to hear the testimony, and the case was turned over to the auxiliary justice, who promptly decided in the manner desired by the authorities. Mercado at once took an appeal, but the venal Weyler moved a force of artillery to Kalamba and quartered it upon the town as if rebellion openly existed there. Then the court representatives evicted the people from their homes and directed them to remove all their buildings from the estate lands within twenty-four hours. In answer to the plea that they had appealed to the Supreme Court the tenants were told their houses could be brought back again if they won their appeal. Of course this was impossible and some 150,000 pesos' worth of property was consequently destroyed by the court agents, who were worthy estate employees. Twenty or more families were made homeless and the other tenants were forbidden to shelter them under pain of their own eviction. This is the proceeding in which Retana suggests that the governorgeneral and the landlords were legally within their rights. If so, Spanish law was a disgrace to the nation. Fortunately the Rizal-Mercado family had another piece of property at Los Baños, and there they made their home.

Weyler's motives in this matter do not have to be surmised, for among the (formerly) secret records of the government there exists a letter which he wrote when he first denied the petition of the Kalamba residents. It is marked "confidential" and is addressed to the landlords, expressing the pleasure which this action gave him. Then the official adds that it cannot have escaped their notice that the times demand diplomacy in handling the situation but that, should occasion arise, he will act with energy. Just as Weyler had favored the landlords at first so he kept on and when he had a chance to do something for them he did it.

Finally, when Weyler left the Islands an investigation was ordered into his administration, owing to rumors of extensive and systematic frauds on the government, but nothing more came of the case than that Retana, later Rizal's biographer, wrote a book in the General's defense, "extensively documented," and also abusively antiFilipino. It has been urged (not by Retana, however) that the Weyler régime was unusually efficient, because he would allow no one but himself to make profits out of the public, and therefore, while his gains were greater than those of his predecessors, the Islands really received more attention from him.

During the Kalamba discussion in Spain,
Retana, until 1899 always scurrilously antiFilipino, made the mistake of his life, for he charged Rizal's family with not paying their rent, which was not true. While Rizal believed that duelling was murder, to judge from a pair of pictures preserved in his album, he evidently considered that homicide of one like Retana was justifiable. After the Spanish custom, his seconds immediately called upon the author of the libel. Retana notes in his "Vida del Dr. Rizal" that the incident closed in a way honorable to both Rizal and himself—he, Retana, published an explicit retraction and abject apology in the Madrid papers. Another time, in Madrid,
Rizal risked a duel when he challenged Antonio Luna, later the General, because of a slighting allusion to a lady at a public banquet. He had a nicer sense of honor in such matters than prevailed in Madrid, and Luna promptly saw the matter from Rizal's point of view and withdrew the offensive remark. This second incident complements the first, for it shows that Rizal was as willing to risk a duel with his superior in arms as with one not so skilled as he. Rizal was an exceptional pistol shot and a fair swordsman, while Retana was inferior with either sword

or pistol, but Luna, who would have had the choice of weapons, was immeasurably Rizal's superior with the sword.

Owing to a schism a rival arose against the old Masonry and finally the original organization succumbed to the offshoot. Doctor Miguel Morayta, Professor of History in the Central University at Madrid, was the head of the new institution and it had grown to be very popular among students. Doctor Morayta was friendly to the Filipinos and a lodge of the same name as their paper was organized among them. For their outside work they had a society named the HispanoFilipino Association, of which Morayta was president, with convenient clubrooms and a membership practically the same as the Lodge La Solidaridad.

Just before Christmas of 1890, this HispanoFilipino Association gave a largely attended banquet at which there were many prominent speakers. Rizal stayed away, not because of growing pessimism, as Retana suggests, but because one of the speakers was the same Becerra who had feared to act when the outrage against the body of Rizal's brother-inlaw had been reported to him. Now out of office, the ex-minister was again bold in words, but Rizal for one was not again to be deceived by them.

The propaganda carried on by his countrymen in the Peninsula did not seem to Rizal effective, and he found his suggestions were not well received by those at its head. The story of Rizal's separation from La Solidaridad, however, is really not material, but the following quotation from a letter written to Carlos Oliver, speaking of the opposition of the Madrid committee of Filipinos to himself, is interesting as showing Rizal's attitude of mind:

"I regret exceedingly that they war against me, attempting to discredit me in the Philippines, but I shall be content provided only that my successor keeps on with the work. I ask only of those who say that I created discord among the Filipinos: Was there any effective union before I entered political life? Was there any chief whose authority I wanted to oppose? It is a pity that in our slavery we should have rivalries over leadership."

And in Rizal's letter from Hongkong, May 24, 1892, to Zulueta, commenting on an article by Leyte in La Solidaridad, he says:

"Again I repeat, I do not understand the reason of the attack, since now I have dedicated myself to preparing for our countrymen a safe refuge in case of persecution and to writing some books, championing our cause, which shortly will appear. Besides, the article is impolitic in the extreme and prejudicial to the Philippines. Why say that the first thing we need is to have money? A wiser man would be silent and not wash soiled linen in public."

Early in '91 Rizal went to Paris, visiting Mr. Baustead's villa in Biarritz en route, and he was again a guest of his hospitable friend when, after the winter season was over, the family returned to their home in Brussels.

During most of the year Rizal's residence was in Ghent, where he had gathered around him a number of Filipinos. Doctor Blumentritt suggested that he should devote himself to the study of Malay-Polynesian languages, and as it appeared that thus he could earn a living in Holland he thought to make his permanent home there. But his parents were old and reluctant to leave their native land to pass their last years in a strange country, and that plan failed.

He now occupied himself in finishing the sequel to "Noli Me Tangere," the novel "El Filibusterismo," which he had begun in
October of 1887 while on his visit to the Philippines. The bolder painting of the evil effects of the Spanish culture upon the Filipinos may well have been inspired by his unfortunate experiences with his countrymen in Madrid who had not seen anything of Europe outside of Spain. On the other hand, the confidence of the author in those of his countrymen who had not been contaminated by the so-called Spanish civilization, is even more noticeable than in "Noli Me Tangere." Rizal had now done all that he could for his country; he had shown them by Morga what they were when Spain found them; through "Noli Me Tangere" he had painted their condition after three hundred years of Spanish influence; and in "El

Filibusterismo" he had pictured what their future must be if better counsels did not prevail in the colony.

These works were for the instruction of his countrymen, the fulfilment of the task he set for himself when he first read Doctor Jagor's criticism fifteen years before; time only was now needed for them to accomplish their work and for education to bring forth its fruits.

CHAPTER VIII

Despujol's Duplicity

As soon as he had set in motion what influence he possessed in Europe for the relief of his relatives, Rizal hurried to Hongkong and from there wrote to his parents asking their permission to join them. Some time before, his brother-in-law, Manuel Hidalgo, had been deported upon the recommendation of the governor of La Laguna, "to prove to the Filipinos that they were mistaken in thinking that the new Civil Code gave them any rights" in cases where the governor-general agreed with his subordinate's reason for asking for the deportation as well as in its desirability. The offense was having buried a child, who had died of cholera, without church ceremonies. The law prescribed and public health demanded it. But the law was a dead letter and the public health was never considered when these cut into church revenues, as Hidalgo ought to have known.

Upon Rizal's arrival in Hongkong, in the fall of 1891, he received notice that his brother Paciano had been returned from exile in Mindoro, but that three of his sisters had been summoned, with the probability of deportation.

A trap to get Rizal into the hands of the government by playing upon his affection for his mother was planned at this time, but it failed. Mrs. Rizal and one of her daughters were arrested in Manila for "falsification of cedula" because they no longer used the name Realonda, which the mother had dropped fifteen years before. Then, though there were frequently boats running to Kalamba, the two women were ordered to be taken there for trial on foot. As when Mrs. Rizal had been a prisoner before, the humane guards disobeyed their orders and the elderly lady was carried in a hammock. The family understood the plans of their persecutors, and Rizal was told by his parents not to come to Manila. Then the persecution of the mother and the sister dropped.

In Hongkong, Rizal was already acquainted with most of the Filipino colony, including Jose M. Basa, a '72 exile of great energy, for whom he had the greatest respect. The old man was an unceasing enemy of all the religious orders and was constantly getting out "proclamations," as the handbills common in the old-time controversies were called. One of these, against the Jesuits, figures in the case against Rizal and bears some minor corrections in his handwriting. Nevertheless, his participation in it was probably no more than this proofreading for his friend, whose motives he could appreciate, but whose plan of action was not in harmony with his own ideas.

Letters of introduction from London friends secured for Rizal the acquaintance of Mr. H. L. Dalrymple, a justice of the peace—which is a position more coveted and honored in English lands than here—and a member of the public library committee, as well as of the board of medical examiners. He was a merchant, too, and agent for the British North Borneo Company, which had recently secured a charter as a semiindependent colony for the extensive cession which had originally been made to the American Trading Company and later transferred to them.

Rizal spent much of his time in the library, reading especially the files of the older newspapers, which contained frequent mention of the Philippines. As an oldtime missionary had left his books to the library, the collection was rich in writings of the fathers of the early Church, as well as in philology and travel. He spent much time also in long conversations with Editor FrazierSmith of the Hongkong Telegraph, the

most enterprising of the daily newspapers. He was the master of St. John's Masonic lodge (Scotch constitution), which Rizal had visited upon his first arrival, intensely democratic and a close student of world politics. The two became fast friends and Rizal contributed to the Telegraph several articles on Philippine matters. These were printed in Spanish, ostensibly for the benefit of the Filipino colony in Hongkong, but large numbers of the paper were mailed to the Philippines and thus at first escaped the vigilance of the censors. Finally the scheme was discovered and the Telegraph placed on the prohibited list, but, like most Spanish actions, this was just too late to prevent the circulation of what Rizal had wished to say to his countrymen.
With the first of the year 1892 the free portion of Rizal's family came to Hongkong. He had been licensed to practice medicine in the colony, and opened an office, specializing as an oculist with notable success.

Another congenial companion was a man of his own profession, Doctor L. P. Marquez, a Portuguese who had received his medical education in Dublin and was a naturalized British subject. He was a leading member of the Portuguese club, Lusitania, which was of radically republican proclivities and possessed an excellent library of books on modern political conditions. An inspection of the colonial prison with him inspired Rizal's article, "A Visit to Victoria Gaol," through which runs a pathetic contrast of the English system of imprisonment for reformation with the Spanish vindictive methods of punishment. A souvenir of one of their many conferences was a dainty modeling in clay made by Rizal with that astonishing quickness that resulted from his Uncle Gabriel's training during his early childhood.

In the spring, Rizal took a voyage to British North Borneo and with Mr. Pryor, the agent, looked over vacant lands which had been offered him by the Company for a Filipino colony. The officials were anxious to grow abaca, cacao, sugar cane and coconuts, all products of the Philippines, the soil of which resembled theirs. So they welcomed the prospect of the immigration of laborers skilled in such cultivation, the Kalambans and other persecuted people of the Luzon lake region, whom Doctor Rizal hoped to transplant there to a freer home.

A different kind of governor-general had succeeded Weyler in the Philippines; the new man was Despujol, a friend of the Jesuits and a man who at once gave the Filipinos hope of better days, for his promises were quickly backed up by the beginnings of their performance. Rizal witnessed this novel experience for his country with gratification, though he had seen too many disappointments to confide in the continuance of reform, and he remembered that the like liberal term of De la Torre had ended in the Cavite reaction.

He wrote early to the new chief executive, applauding Despujol's policy and offering such coöperation as he might be able to give toward making it a complete success. No reply had been received, but after Rizal's return from his Borneo trip the Spanish consul in Hongkong assured him that he would not be molested should he go to Manila.

Rizal therefore made up his mind to visit his home once more. He still cherished the plan of transferring those of his relatives and friends who were homeless through the land troubles, or discontented with their future in the Philippines, to the district offered to him by the British North Borneo Company. There, under the protection of the British flag, but in their accustomed climate, with familiar surroundings amid their own people, a New Kalamba would be established. Filipinos would there have a chance to prove to the world what they were capable of, and their free condition would inevitably react on the neighboring Philippines and help to bring about better government there.

Rizal had no intention of renouncing his Philippine allegiance, for he always regretted the naturalization of his countrymen abroad, considering it a loss to the country which needed numbers to play the influential part he hoped it would play in awakening Asia. All his arguments were for British justice and "Equality before the Law," for he considered that political power was only a means of securing and assuring fair treatment for all, and in itself of no interest.

With such ideas he sailed for home, bearing the Spanish consul's passport. He left two letters in Hongkong with his friend Doctor Marquez marked, "To be opened after my death," and their contents indicate that he was not unmindful of how little regard Spain had had in his country for her plighted honor.

One was to his beloved parents, brother and sisters, and friends:

"The affection that I have ever professed for you suggests this step, and time alone can tell whether or not it is sensible. Their outcome decides things by results, but whether that be favorable or unfavorable, it may always be said that duty urged me, so if I die in doing it, it will not matter.

"I realize how much suffering I have caused you, still I do not regret what I have done. Rather, if I had to begin over again, still I should do just the same, for it has been only duty. Gladly do I go to expose myself to peril, not as any expiation of misdeeds (for in this matter I believe myself guiltless of any), but to complete my work and myself offer the example of which I have always preached.

"A man ought to die for duty and his principles. I hold fast to every idea which I have advanced as to the condition and future of our country, and shall willingly die for it, and even more willingly to procure for you justice and peace.

"With pleasure, then, I risk life to save so many innocent persons—so many nieces and nephews, so many children of friends, and children, too, of others who are not even friends—who are suffering on my account. What am I? A single man, practically without family, and sufficiently undeceived as to life. I have had many disappointments and the future before me is gloomy, and will be gloomy if light does not illuminate it, the dawn of a better day for my native land. On the other hand, there are many individuals, filled with hope and ambition, who perhaps all might be happy were I dead, and then I hope my enemies would be satisfied and stop persecuting so many entirely innocent people. To a certain extent their hatred is justifiable as to myself, and my parents and relatives.

"Should fate go against me, you will all understand that I shall die happy in the thought that my death will end all your troubles. Return to our country and may you be happy in it.

"Till the last moment of my life I shall be thinking of you and wishing you all good fortune and happiness."

* * * * *

The other letter was directed "To the Filipinos," and said:

"The step which I am taking, or rather am about to take, is undoubtedly risky, and it is unnecessary to say that I have considered it some time. I understand that almost every one is opposed to it; but I know also that hardly anybody else comprehends what is in my heart. I cannot live on seeing so many suffer unjust persecutions on my account; I cannot bear longer the sight of my sisters and their numerous families treated like criminals. I prefer death and cheerfully shall relinquish life to free so many innocent persons from such unjust persecution.

"I appreciate that at present the future of our country gravitates in some degree around me, that at my death many will feel triumphant, and, in consequence, many are wishing for my fall. But what of it? I hold duties of conscience above all else, I have obligations to the families who suffer, to my aged parents whose sighs strike me to the heart; I know that I alone, only with my death, can make them happy, returning them to their native land and to a peaceful life at home. I am all my parents have, but our country has many, many more sons who can take my place and even do my work better.

"Besides I wish to show those who deny us patriotism that we know how to die for duty and principles. What matters death, if one dies for what one loves, for native land and beings held dear?

"If I thought that I were the only resource for the policy of progress in the Philippines and were I convinced that my countrymen were going to make use of my services, perhaps I should hesitate about taking this step; but there are still others who can take my place, who, too, can take my place with advantage. Furthermore, there are perchance those who hold me unneeded and my services are not utilized, resulting that I am reduced to inactivity.

"Always have I loved our unhappy land, and I am sure that I shall continue loving it till my latest moment, in case men prove unjust to me. My career, my life, my happiness, all have I sacrificed for love of it. Whatever my fate, I shall die blessing it and longing for the dawn of its redemption."

And then followed the note; "Make these letters public after my death."

Suspicion of the Spanish authorities was justified. The consul's cablegram notifying Governor-General Despujol. that Rizal had fallen into their trap, sent the day of issuing the "safe-conduct" or special passport, bears the same date as the secret case filed against him in Manila, "for anti religious and anti patriotic agitation." On that same day the deceitful Despujol was confidentially inquiring of his executive secretary whether it was true that Rizal had been naturalized as a German subject, and, if so, what effect would that have on the governorgeneral's right to take executive action; that is, could he deport one who had the protection of a strong nation with the same disregard for the forms of justice that he could a Filipino?

This inquiry is joined to an order to the local authorities in the provinces near Manila instructing them to watch the comings and goings of their prominent people during the following weeks. The scheme resembled that which was concocted prior to '72, but Governor-General de la Torte was honest in his reforms. Despujol may, or may not, have been honest in other matters, but as concerns Rizal there is no lack of proof of his perfidy. The confidential file relating to this part of the case was forgotten in destroying and removing secret papers when Manila passed into a democratic conqueror's hands, and now whoever wishes may read, in the Bureau of Archives, documents which the Conde de Caspe, to use a noble title for an ignoble man, considered safely hidden. As with Weyler's contidential letter to the friar landlords, these discoveries convict their writers of bad faith, with no possibility of mistake.

This point in the reformed Spanish writer's biography of Rizal is made occasion for another of his treacherous attacks upon the good name of his pretended hero. Just as in the land troubles Retana held that legally Governor-General Weyler was justified in disregarding an appeal pending in the courts, so in this connection he declares: "(Despujol) unquestionably had been deceived by Rizal when, from Hongkong, he offered to Despujol not to meddle in politics." That
Rizal meddled in politics rests solely upon Despujol's word, and it will be seen later how little that is worth; but, politics or no politics, Rizal's fate was settled before he ever came to Manila.

Rizal was accompanied to Manila by his sister Lucia, widow of that brother-in-law who had been denied Christian burial because of his relationship to Rizal. In the Basa home, among other waste papers, and for that use, she had gathered up five copies of a recent "proclamation," entitled "Pobres Frailes" (Poor Friars), a small sheet possibly two inches wide and five long. These, crumpled up, were tucked into the case of the pillow which Mrs. Hervosa used on board. Later, rolled up in her blankets and bed mat, or petate, they went to the custom house along with the other baggage, and of course were discovered in the rigorous examination which the officers always made. How strict Philippine customs searches were, Henry Norman, an English writer of travels, explains by remarking that Manila was the only port where he had ever had his pockets picked officially. His visit was made at about the time of which we are writing, and the object, he says, was to keep out anti friar publications.

Rizal and his sister landed without difficulty, and he at once went to the Oriente Hotel, then the best in town, for Rizal always traveled and lived as became a member of a well-todo family. Next he waited on the

GovernorGeneral, with whom he had a very brief interview, for it happened to be on one of the numerous religious festivals, during which he obtained favorable consideration for his deported sisters. Several more interviews occurred in which the hopes first given were realized, so that those of the family then awaiting exile were pardoned and those already deported were to be returned at an early date.

One night Rizal was the guest of honor at a dinner given by the masters and wardens of the Masonic lodges of Manila, and he was surprised and delighted at the progress the institution had made in the Islands. Then he had another task not so agreeable, for, while awaiting a delayed appointment with the Governor-General, he with two others ran up on the new railway to Tarlac. Ostensibly this was to see the country, but it was not for a pleasure trip. They were investigating the sales of Rizal's books and trying to find out what had become of the money received from them, for while the author's desire had been to place them at so low a price as to be within the reach of even the poor, it was reported that the sales had been few and at high prices, so that copies were only read by the wealthy whose desire to obtain the rare and muchdiscussed novels led them to pay exorbitant figures for them.

Rizal's party, consisting of the Secretary of one of the lodges of Manila, and another Mason, a prominent school-teacher, were under constant surveillance and a minute record of their every act is preserved in the "reserved" files, now, of course, so only in name, as they are no longer secret. Immediately after they left a house it would be thoroughly searched and the occupants strictly questioned. In spite of the precautions of the officials, Rizal soon learned of this, and those whom they visited were warned of what to expect. In one home so many forbidden papers were on hand that Rizal delayed his journey till the family completed their task of carrying them upstairs and hiding them in the roof.

At another place he came across an instance of superstition such as that which had caused him to cease his sleight-of-hand exhibitions on his former return to the Islands. Their host was a man of little education but great hospitality, and the party were most pleasantly entertained. During the conversation he spoke of Rizal, but did not seem to know that his hero had come back to the Philippines. His remarks drifted into the wildest superstition, and, after asserting that Rizal bore a charmed life, he startled his audience by saying that if the author of "Noli Me Tangere" cared to do so, he could be with them at that very instant. At first the three thought themselves discovered by their host, but when Rizal made himself known, the old man proved that he had had no suspicion of his guest's identity, for he promptly became busy preparing his home for the search which he realized would shortly follow. On another occasion their host was a stranger whom Rizal treated for a temporary illness, leaving a prescription to be filled at the drug store. The name signed to the paper was a revelation, but the first result was activity in cleaning house.

No fact is more significant of the utter rottenness of the Spanish rule than the unanimity of the people in their discontent. Only a few persons at first were in open opposition, but books, pamphlets and circulars were eagerly sought, read and preserved, with the knowledge generally, of the whole family, despite the danger of possessing them. At times, as in the case of Rizal's novels, an entire neighborhood was in the secret; the book was buried in a garden and dug up to be read from at a gathering of the older men, for which a dance gave pretext. Informers were so rare that the possibility of treachery among themselves was hardly reckoned in the risk.

The authorities were constantly searching dwellings, often entire neighborhoods, and with a thoroughness which entirely disregarded the possibility of damaging an innocent person's property. These "domiciliary registrations" were, of course, supposed to be unexpected, but in the later Spanish days the intended victims usually had warning from some employee in the office where it was planned, or from some domestic of the official in charge; very often, however, the warning was so short as to give only time for a hasty destruction of incriminating documents and did not permit of their being transferred to other hiding places. Thus large losses were incurred, and to these must be added damages from dampness when a hole in the ground, the inside of a post, or cementing up in the wall furnished the means of concealment. Fires, too, were frequent, and such events attracted so much attention that it was scarcely safe to attempt to save anything of an incriminating nature.

Six years of war conditions did their part toward destroying what little had escaped, and from these explanations the reader may understand how it comes that the tangled story of Spain's last half century here presents an historical problem more puzzling than that of much more remote times in more favored lands.

It seems almost providential that the published statement of the Governor-General can be checked not only by an account which Rizal secretly sent to friends, but also by the candid memoranda contained in the untruthful executive's own secret folios. While some unessential details of Rizal's career are in doubt, not a point vital to establishing his good name lacks proof that his character was exemplary and that he is worthy of the hero-worship which has come to him.

After Rizal's return to Manila from his railway trip he had the promised interview with the Governor-General. At their previous meetings the discussions had been quite informal. Rizal, in complimenting the General upon his inauguration of reforms, mentioned that the Philippine system of having no restraint whatever upon the chief executive had at least the advantage that a well-disposed governor-general would find no red-tape hindrances to his plans for the public benefit. But Despujol professed to believe that the best of men make mistakes and that a wise government would establish safeguards against this human fallibility.

The final, and fatal, interview began with the Governor-General asking Rizal if he still persisted in his plan for a Filipino colony in British North Borneo; Despujol had before remarked that with so much Philippine land lying idle for want of cultivation it did not seem to him patriotic to take labor needed at home away for the development of a foreign land. Rizal's former reply had dealt with the difficulty the government was in respecting the land troubles, since the tenants who had taken the old renters' places now also must be considered, and he pointed out that there was, besides, a bitterness between the parties which could not easily be forgotten by either side. So this time he merely remarked that he had found no reason for changing his original views.

Hereupon the General took from his desk the five little sheets of the "Poor Friars" handbill, which he said had been found in the roll of bedding sent with Rizal's baggage to the custom house, and asked whose they could be. Rizal answered that of course the General knew that the bedding belonged to his sister Lucia, but she was no fool and would not have secreted in a place where they were certain to be found five little papers which, hidden within her camisa or placed in her stocking, would have been absolutely sure to come in unnoticed.

Rizal, neither then nor later, knew the real truth, which was that these papers were gathered up at random and without any knowledge of their contents. If it was a crime to have lived in a house where such seditious printed matter was common, then Rizal, who had openly visited Basa's home, was guilty before ever the handbills were found. But no reasonable person would believe another rational being could be so careless of consequences as to bring in openly such dangerous material.

The very title was in sarcastic allusion to the inconsistency of a religious order being an immensely wealthy organization, while its individual members were vowed to poverty. News, published everywhere except in the Philippines, of losses sustained in outside commercial enterprises running into the millions, was made the text for showing how money, professedly raised in the Philippines for charities, was not so used and was invested abroad in fear of that day of reckoning when tyranny would be overthrown in anarchy and property would be insecure. The belief of the pious Filipinos, fostered by their religious exploiters, that the Pope would suffer great hardship if their share of "Peter's pence" was not prompt and full, was contrasted with another newspaper story of a rich dowry given to a favorite niece by a former Pope, but that in no way taught the truth that the Head of the Church was not put to bodily discomfort whenever a poor Filipino failed to come forward with his penny.

Despujol managed to work himself into something like a passion over this alleged disrespect to the Pope, and ordered Rizal to be taken as a prisoner to Fort Santiago by the nephew who acted as his aide.

Like most facts, this version runs a middle course between the extreme stories which have been current. Like circulars may have been printed at the "Asilo de Malabon," as has been asserted; these certainly came from Hongkong and were not introduced by any archbishop's nephew on duty at the custom house, as another tale suggests. On the other hand, the circular was the merest pretext, and Despujol did not act in good faith, as many claim that he did.

It may be of interest to reprint the handbill from a facsimile of an original copy:

Pobres Frailes!

Acaba de suspender sus pages un Banco,
acaba de quebrarse el New Oriental.

Grandes pédidas en la India, en la isla Mauricio al sur de Africa, ciclónes y tempestades acabaron con su podeíro, tragnádose más de 36,000,000 de pesos. Estos treinta y seis millones representaban las esperanzas, las economías, el bienestar y el porvenir de numerosos individuos y familias.

Entre los que más han sufrido podemos contar á la Rvda. Corporacion de los P. P.

Dominicos, que pierden en esta quiebra muchos cientos de miles. No se sabe la cuenta exacta porque tanto dinero se les envía de aquí y tantos depósitos hacen, que se neçesitarlan muchos contadores para calcular el immense caudal de que disponen.

Pero, no se aflijan los amigos ni triunfen los enemigos de los santos monjes que profesan vote de pobreza.

A unos y otros les diremos que pueden estar tranquilos. La Corporacion tiene aun muchos millones depositados en los Bancos de Hongkong, y aunque todos quebrasen, y aunque se derrumbasen sus miles de casas de alquiler, siempre quedarian sus curates y haciendas, les quedarían los filipinos dispuestos siempre á ayunar para darles una limosna. ¿Qué son cuatrocientos ó quinientos mil? Que se tomen la molestia de recorrer los pueblos y pedir limosna y se resarcirán de esa pérdida. Hace un año que, por la mala administracion de los cardenales, el Papa perdió 14,000,000 del dinero de San Pedro; el Papa, para cubrir el déficit, acude á nosotros

y nosotros recogemos de nuestros tampipis el último real, porque sabemos que el Papa tiene muchas atenciones; hace cosa de cinco años casó á una sobrina suya dotándola de un palacio y 300,000 francos ademas. Haced un esfuerzo pues, generosos filipinos, y socorred á los dominicos igualmente!

Además, esos centanares de miles perdidos no son de ellos, segun dicen: ¿cómo los iban à tener si tienen voto de pobreza? Hay que creerlos pues cuando, para cubrirse, dicen que son de los huérfanos y de las viudas. Muy seguramente pertencerían algunos á las viudas y á los huérfanos de Kalamba, y quién sabe si á los desterrados maridos! y los manejan los virtuosos frailes sólo á título de depositarios para devolverlos despues religiosamente con todos sus intereses cuando llegue el día de rendir cuentas! Quién sabe? Quién mejor que ellos podía encargarse de recoger los pocos haberes mientras las casas ardían, huían las viudas y los huérfanos sin encontrar hospitalidad, pues se habia prohibido darles albergue, mientras los hombres estaban presos ó perseguidos? ¿Quién mejor que los dominicos para tener tanto valor, tanta audacia y tanta humanidad?

Pero, ahora el diablo se ha llevado el dinero de los huérfanos y de las viudas, y es de temer que se lleve tambien el resto, pues cuando el diablo la empieza la ha de acabar. Tendría ese dinero mala procedencia?

Si asl sucediese, nosotros los recomendaríamos á los dominicos que dijesen con Job: Desnudo salí del vientre de mi madre (España), y desnudo volveré allá; lo dió el diablo, el diablo se lo llevó; bendito sea el nombre del Señor!

Fr. Jacinto.

Manila: Imprenta de los Amigos del Pais.

CHAPTER IX

The Deportation to Dapitan

As soon as Rizal was lodged in his prison, a room in Fort Santiago, the Governor-General began the composition of one of the most extraordinary official documents ever issued in this land where the strangest governmental acts have abounded. It is apology, argument, and attack all in one and was published in the Official Gazette, where it occupied most of an entire issue. The effect of the righteous anger it displays suffers somewhat when one knows how all was planned from the day Rizal was decoyed from Hongkong under the faithless safeconduct. Another enlightening feature is the copy of a later letter, preserved in that invaluable secret file, wherein Despujol writes Rizal's custodian, as jailer, to allow the exile in no circumstances to see this number of the Gazette or to know its contents, and suggests several evasions to assist the subordinate's power of invention. It is certainly a strange indignation which fears that its object shall learn the reason for wrath, nor is it a creditable spectacle when one beholds the chief of a government giving private lessons in lying.
A copy of the Gazette was sent to the Spanish Consul in Hongkong, also a cablegram directing him to give it publicity that "Spain's good name might not suffer" in that colony. By his blunder, not knowing that the Lusitania Club was really a Portuguese Masonic lodge and full of Rizal's

friends, a copy was sent there and a strong reply was called forth. The friendly editor of the
Hongkong Telegraph devoted columns to the outrage by which a man whose acquaintance in the scientific world reflected honor upon his nation, was decoyed to what was intended to be his death, exiled to "an unhealthful, savage spot," through "a plot of which the very Borgias would have been ashamed."

The British Consul in Manila, too, mentioned unofficially to GovernorGeneral Despujol that it seemed a strange way of showing Spain's often professed friendship for Great
Britain thus to disregard the annoyance to the British colony of North Borneo caused by making impossible an entirely unexceptionable plan. Likewise, in much the same respectfully remonstrant tone which the Great Powers are wont to use in recalling to semi-savage states their obligations to civilization, he pointed out how Spain's prestige as an advanced nation would suffer when the educated world, in which Rizal was Spain's best-known representative, learned that the man whom they honored had been trapped out of his security under the British flag and sent into exile without the slightest form of trial.

Almost the last act of Rizal while at liberty was the establishment of the "Liga Filipina," a league or association seeking to unite all Filipinos of good character for concerted action toward the economic advancement of their country, for a higher standard of manhood, and to assure opportunities for education and development to talented Filipino youth. Resistance to oppression by lawful means was also urged, for Rizal believed that no one could fairly complain of bad government until he had exhausted and found unavailing all the legal resources provided for his protection. This was another expression of his constant teaching that slaves, those who toadied to power, and men without self-respect made possible and fostered tyranny, abuses and disregard of the rights of others.

The character test was also a step forward, for the profession of patriotism has often been made to cloak moral shortcomings in the

Philippines as well as elsewhere. Rizal urged that those who would offer themselves on the altar of their fatherland must conform to the standard of old, and, like the sacrificial lamb, be spotless and without blemish. Therefore, no one who had justifiably been prosecuted for any infamous crime was eligible to membership in the new organization.

The plan, suggested by a Spanish Masonic society called C. Kadosch y Cia., originated with José Maria Basa, at whose instance Rizal drafted the constitution and regulations. Possibly all the members were Freemasons of the educated and better-to-do class, and most of them adhered to the doctrine that peaceably obtained reforms and progress by education are surest and best.

Rizal's arrest discouraged those of this higher faith, for the peaceable policy seemed hopeless, while the radical element, freed from Rizal's restraining influence and deeming the time for action come, formed a new and revolutionary society which preached force of arms as the only argument left to them, and sought its membership among the lessenlightened and poorer class.

Their inspiration was Andrés Bonifacio, a shipping clerk for a foreign firm, who had read and re-read accounts of the French Revolution till he had come to believe that blood alone could wipe out the wrongs of a country. His organization, The Sons of the Country, more commonly called the Katipunan, was, however, far from being as bloodthirsty as most Spanish accounts, and those of many credulous writers who have got their ideas from them, have asserted. To enlist others in their defense, those who knew that they were the cause of dissatisfaction spread the report that a race war was in progress and that the Katipuneros were planning the massacre of all of the white race.

It was a sufficiently absurd statement, but it was made even more ridiculous by its "proof," for this was the discovery of an apron with a severed head, a hand holding it by the hair and another grasping the dagger which had done the bloody work. This emblem, handed down from ancient days as an object lesson of faithfulness even to death, has been known in many lands besides the Philippines, but only here has it ever been considered anything but an ancient symbol. As reasonably might the paintings of martyrdoms in the convents be taken as evidence of evil intentions upon the part of their occupants, but prejudice looks for pretexts rather than reasons, and this served as well as any other for the excesses of which the government in its frenzy of fear was later guilty.

In talking of the Katipunan one must distinguish the first society, limited in its membership, from the organization of the days of the Aguinaldo "republic," so called, when throughout the Tagalog provinces, and in the chief towns of other provinces as well, adherence to the revolutionary government entailed membership in the revolutionary society. And neither of these two Katipunans bore any relation, except in name and emblems, to the robber bands whose valor was displayed after the war had ceased and whose patriotism consisted in wronging and robbing their own defenseless countrymen and countrywomen, while carefully avoiding encounters with any able to defend themselves.

Rizal's arrest had put an end to all hope of progress under GovernorGeneral Despujol. It had left the political field in possession of those countrymen who had not been in sympathy with his campaign of education. It had caused the succession of the revolutionary Katipunan to the economic Liga Filipina, with talk of independence supplanting Rizal's ambition for the return of the Philippines to their former status under the Constitution of Cadiz. But the victim of the arrest was at peace as he had not been in years. The sacrifice for country and for family had been made, but it was not to cost him life, and he was human enough to wish to live. A visitor's room in the Fort and books from the military library made his detention comfortable, for he did not worry about the Spanish sentries without his door who were placed there under orders to shoot anyone who might attempt to signal to him from the plaza.

One night the Governor-General's nephewaide came again to the Fort and Rizal embarked on the steamer which was to take him to his place of exile, but closely as he was guarded he risked dropping a note which a

Filipino found and took, as it directed, to Mrs. Rizal's cousin, Vicenta Leyba, who lived in Calle José, Trozo. Thus the family were advised of his departure; this incident shows Rizal's perfect confidence in his countrymen and the extent to which it was justified; he could risk a chance finder to take so dangerous a letter to its address.

On the steamer he occupied an officer's cabin and also found a Filipino quartermaster, of whom he requested a life preserver for his stateroom; evidently he was not entirely confident that there were no hostile designs against him. Accidents had rid the Philippines of troublesome persons before his time, and he was determined that if he sacrificed his life for his country, it should be openly. He realized that the tree of Liberty is often watered with the blood of secret as well as open martyrs.

The same boat carried some soldier prisoners, one of whom was to be executed in Mindanao, and their case was not particularly creditable to Spanish ideas of justice. A Spanish officer had dishonorably interfered with the domestic relations of a sergeant, also Spanish, and the aggrieved party had inflicted punishment upon his superior, with the help of some other soldiers. For allowing himself to be punished, not for his own disgraceful act, the officer was dismissed from the service, but the sergeant was to go to the scene of his alleged "crime," there to suffer death, while his companions who had assisted him in protecting their homes were to be witnesses of this "justice" and then to be imprisoned.

After an uneventful trip the steamer reached

Dapitan, in the northeast of the large island of Mindanao, on a dark and rainy evening. The officer in charge of the expedition took Doctor Rizal ashore with some papers relating to him and delivered all to the commandant, Ricardo Carnicero. The receipt taken was briefed "One countryman and two packages." At the same time learned men in Europe were beginning to hear of this outrage worthy of the Dark Ages and were remarking that Spain had stopped the work of the man who was practically her only representative in modern science, for the Castilian language has not been the medium through which any considerable additions have been made to the world's store of scientific knowledge.

Rizal was to reside either with the commandant or with the Jesuit parish priest, if the latter would take him into the convento. But while the exile had learned with pleasure that he was to meet priests who were refined and learned, as well as associated with his happier school days, he did not know that these priests were planning to restore him to his childhood faith and had mapped out a plan of action which should first make him feel his loneliness. So he was denied residence with the priest unless he would declare himself genuinely in sympathy with Spain.

On his previous brief visit to the Islands he had been repelled from the Ateneo with the statement that till he ceased to be antiCatholic and antiSpanish he would not be welcome. Padre Faura, the famous meteorologist, was his former instructor and Rizal was his favorite pupil; he had tearfully predicted that the young man would come to the scaffold at last unless he mended his ways. But Rizal, confident in the clearness of his own conscience, went out cheerfully, and when the porter tried to bring back the memory of his childhood piety by reminding him of the image of the Sacred Heart which he had carved years before, Rizal answered, "Other times, other customs, Brother. I do not believe that way any more."

So Rizal, a good Catholic, was compelled to board with the commandant instead of with the priest because he was unwilling to make hypocritical professions of admiration for Spain. The commandant and Rizal soon became good friends, but in order to retain his position Carnicero had to write to the Governor-General in a different strain.

The correspondence tells the facts in the main, but of course they are colored throughout to conform to Despujol's character. The commandant is always represented as deceiving his prisoner and gaining his confidence only to betray him, but Rizal seems never to have experienced anything but straightforward dealing.

Rizal's earliest letter from Dapitan speaks almost enthusiastically of the place, describing the climate as exceptional for the tropics, his situation as agreeable, and saying that he could be quite content if his family and his books were there.

Shortly after occurred the anniversary of Carnicero's arrival in the town, and Rizal celebrated the event with a Spanish poem reciting the improvements made since his coming, written in the style of the Malay loa, and as though it were by the children of Dapitan.

Next Rizal acquired a piece of property at Talisay, a little bay close to Dapitan, and at once became interested in his farm. Soon he built a house and moved into it, gathering a number of boy assistants about him, and before long he had a school. A hospital also was put up for his patients and these in time became a source of revenue, as people from a distance came to the oculist for treatment and paid liberally.

One five-hundred-peso fee from a rich Englishman was devoted by Rizal to lighting the town, and the community benefited in this way by his charity in addition to the free treatment given its poor.

The little settlement at Talisay kept growing and those who lived there were constantly improving it. When Father Obach, the Jesuit priest, fell through the bamboo stairway in the principal house, Rizal and his boys burned shells, made mortar, and soon built a fine stone stairway. They also did another piece of masonry work in the shape of a dam for storing water that was piped to the houses and poultry yard; the overflow from the dam was made to fill a swimming tank.

The school, including the house servants, numbered about twenty and was taught without books by Rizal, who conducted his recitations from a hammock. Considerable importance was given to mathematics, and in languages English was taught as well as Spanish, the entire waking period being devoted to the language allotted for the day, and whoever so far forgot as to utter a word in any other tongue was punished by having to wear a rattan handcuff. The use and meaning of this modern police device had to be explained to the boys, for Spain still tied her prisoners with rope.

Nature study consisted in helping the Doctor gather specimens of flowers, shells, insects and reptiles which were prepared and shipped to German museums. Rizal was paid for these specimens by scientific books and material. The director of the Royal Zoölogical and
Anthropological Museum in Dresden, Saxony, Doctor Karl von Heller, was a great friend and admirer of Doctor Rizal. Doctor Heller's father was tutor to the late King
Alfonso XII and had many friends at the Court of Spain. Evidently Doctor Heller and other of his European friends did not consider Rizal a Spanish insurrectionary, but treated him rather as a reformer seeking progress by peaceful means.

Doctor Rizal remunerated his pupils' work with gifts of clothing, books and other useful remembrances. Sometimes the rewards were cartidges, and those who had accumulated enough were permitted to accompany him in his hunting expeditions. The dignity of labor was practically inculcated by requiring everyone to make himself useful, and this was really the first school of the type, combining the use of English, nature study and industrial instruction.

On one occasion in the year 1894 some of his schoolboys secretly went into the town in a banca; a puppy which tried to follow them was eaten by a crocodile. Rizal tired to impress the evil effects of disobedience upon the youngsters by pointing out to them the sorrow which the mother-dog felt at the loss of her young one, and emphasized the lesson by modeling a statuette called "The Mother's Revenge," wherein she is represented, in revenge, as devouring the cayman. It is said to be a good likeness of the animal which was Doctor Rizal's favorite companion in his many pedestrian excursions around Dapitan.

Father Francisco Sanchez, Rizal's instructor in rhetoric in the Ateneo, made a long visit to Dapitan and brought with him some surveyor's instruments, which his former pupil was delighted to assist him in using.

Together they ran the levels for a water system for the the town, which was later, with the aid of the lay Jesuit, Brother Tildot, carried to completion. This same water

system is now being restored and enlarged with artesian wells by the present insular, provincial and municipal governments jointly, as part of the memorial to Rizal in this place of his exile.

A visit to a not distant mountain and some digging in a spot supposed by the people of the region to be haunted brought to light curious relics of the first Christian converts among the early Moros.

The state of his mind at about this period of his career is indicated by the verses written in his home in Talisay, entitled "My Retreat," of which the following translation has been made by Mr. Charles Derbyshire. The scene that inspired this poem has been converted by the government into a public park to the memory of Rizal.

My Retreat

By the spreading beach where the sands are soft and fine,

At the foot of the mount in its mantle of green,
I have built my hut in the pleasant grove's confine;
From the forest seeking peace and a calmness divine,
Rest for the weary brain and silence to my sorrow keen.

Its roof the frail palm-leaf and its floor the cane,
Its beams and posts of the unhewn wood;
Little there is of value in this hut so plain, And better by far in the lap of the mount to have lain,
By the song and the murmur of the high sea's flood.

A purling brook from the woodland glade Drops down o'er the stones and around it sweeps,
Whence a fresh stream is drawn by the rough cane's aid;

That in the still night its murmur has made,   And in the day's heat a crystal fountain leaps.

When the sky is serene how gently it flows,
And its zither unseen ceaselessly plays;
But when the rains fall a torrent it goes   Boiling and foaming through the rocky close,
Roaring uncheck'd to the sea's wide ways.

The howl of the dog and the song of the bird,
And only the kalao's hoarse call resound;
Nor is the voice of vain man to be heard,
My mind to harass or my steps to begird;   The woodlands alone and the sea wrap me round.

The sea, ah, the sea! for me it is all,
As it massively sweeps from the worlds apart;
Its smile in the morn to my soul is a call,
And when in the even my fath seems to pall,   It breathes with its sadness an echo to my heart.

By night an arcanum; when translucent it glows,
All spangled over with its millions of lights,   And the bright sky above resplendent shows;
While the waves with their sighs tell of their
woes—
Tales that are lost as they roll to the heights.

They tell of the world when the first dawn broke,
And the sunlight over their surface played;   When thousands of beings from nothingness woke,
To people the depths and the heights to cloak,
Wherever its life-giving kiss was laid.

But when in the night the wild winds awake,

And the waves in their fury begin to leap, Through the air rush the cries that my mind shake;
Voices that pray, songs and moans that partake
Of laments from the souls sunk down in the deep.

Then from their heights the mountains groan,

And the trees shiver tremulous from great unto least;
The groves rustle plaintive and the herds utter moan,
For they say that the ghosts of the folk that are gone
Are calling them down to their death's merry feast.

In terror and confusion whispers the night, While blue and green flames flit over the deep;
But calm reigns again with the morning's light,
And soon the bold fisherman comes into sight, As his bark rushes on and the waves sink to sleep.

So onward glide the days in my lonely abode;
Driven forth from the world where once I was known,
I muse o'er the fate upon me bestow'd; A fragment forgotten that the moss will corrode,

To hide from mankind the world in me shown.

I live in the thought of the lov'd ones left,
And oft their names to my mind are borne; Some have forsaken me and some by death are reft;
But now 'tis all one, as through the past I drift,
That past which from me can never be torn.

For it is the friend that is with me always, That ever in sorrow keeps the faith in my soul;
While through the still night it watches and prays,
As here in my exile in my lone hut it stays, To strengthen my faith when doubts o'er me roll.

That faith I keep and I hope to see shine
The day when the Idea prevails over might; When after the fray and death's slow decline,
Some other voice sounds, far happier than mine,

To raise the glad song of the triumph of right.

I see the sky glow, refulgent and clear, As when it forced on me my first dear illusion;
I feel the same wind kiss my forehead sere,
And the fire is the same that is burning here To stir up youth's blood in boiling confusion.

I breathe here the winds that perchance have pass'd
O'er the fields and the rivers of my own natal shore;
And mayhap they will bring on the returning blast
The sighs that lov'd being upon them has cast—
Messages sweet from the love I first bore.

To see the same moon, all silver'd as of yore,
I feel the sad thoughts within me arise; The fond recollections of the troth we swore,

Of the field and the bower and the wide seashore,
The blushes of joy, with the silence and sighs.

A butterfly seeking the flowers and the light,
Of other lands dreaming, of vaster extent; Scarce a youth, from home and love I took flight,
To wander unheeding, free from doubt or affright—

So in foreign lands were my brightest days spent.

And when like a languishing bird I was fain To the home of my fathers and my love to return,
Of a sudden the fierce tempest roar'd amain; So I saw my wings shatter'd and no home remain,

My trust sold to others and wrecks round me burn.

Hurl'd out into exile from the land I adore,
My future all dark and no refuge to seek;
My roseate dreams hover round me once more,
Sole treasures of all that life to me bore; The faiths of youth that with sincerity speak.

But not as of old, full of life and of grace,
Do you hold out hopes of undying reward;
Sadder I find you; on your lov'd face, Though still sincere, the pale lines trace The marks of the faith it is yours to guard.

You offer now, dreams, my gloom to appease,
And the years of my youth again to disclose; So I thank you, O storm, and heaven-born breeze,
That you knew of the hour my wild flight to ease,
To cast me back down to the soil whence I rose.

By the spreading beach where the sands are soft and fine,
At the foot of the mount in its mantle of green;
I have found a home in the pleasant grove's confine,

In the shady woods, that peace and calmness divine,
Rest for the weary brain and silence to my sorrow keen.

The Church benefited by the presence of the exile, for he drew the design for an elaborate curtain to adorn the sanctuary at Easter time, and an artist Sister of Charity of the school there did the oil painting under his direction. In this line he must have been proficient, for once in Spain, where he traveled out of his way to Saragossa to visit one of his former teachers of the Ateneo, who he had heard was there, Rizal offered his assistance in making some altar paintings, and the Jesuit says that his skill and taste were much appreciated.

The home of the Sisters had a private chapel, for which the teachers were preparing an image of the Virgin. For the sake of economy the head only was procured from abroad, the vestments concealing all the rest of the figure except the feet, which rested upon a globe encircled by a snake in whose mouth is an apple. The beauty of the countenance, a real work of art, appealed to Rizal, and he modeled the more prominent right foot, the apple and the serpent's head, while the artist Sister assisted by doing the minor work. Both curtain and image, twenty years after their making, are still in use.

On Sundays, Father Sanchez and Rizal conducted a school for the people after mass. As part of this education it was intended to make raised maps in the plaza of the chief city of the eight principal islands of the Philippines, but on account of Father Sanchez's being called away, only one. Mindanao, was completed; it has been restored with a concrete sidewalk and balustrade about it, while the plaza is a national park.

Among Rizal's patients was a blind American named Taufer, fairly well to do, who had been engineer of the pumping plant of the Hongkong Fire Department. He was a man of bravery, for he held a diploma for helping to rescue five Spaniards from a shipwreck in Hongkong harbor. And he was not less kindhearted, for he and his wife, a Portuguese, had adopted and brought up as their own the infant daughter of a poor Irish woman who had died in Hongkong, leaving a considerable family to her husband, a corporal in the British Army on service there.

The little girl had been educated in the Italian convent after the first Mrs. Taufer died, and upon Mr. Taufer's remarriage, to another Portuguese, the adopted daughter and Mr. Taufer's own child were equally sharers of his home.

This girl had known Rizal, "the Spanish doctor," as he was called there, in Hongkong, and persuaded her adopted father that possibly the Dapitan exile might restore his lost eyesight. So with the two girls and his wife, Mr. Taufer set out for Mindanao. At Manila his own daughter fell in love with a Filipino engineer, a Mr. Sunico, now owner of a foundry in Manila, and, marrying, remained there. But the party reached Dapitan with its original number, for they were joined by a good-looking mestiza from the South who was unofficially connected with one of the canons of the Manila cathedral.

Josefina Bracken, the Irish girl, was lively, capable and of congenial temperament, and as there no longer existed any reason against his marriage, for Rizal considered his political days over, they agreed to become husband and wife.

The priest was asked to perform the ceremony, but said the Bishop of Cebu must give his consent, and offered to write him. Rizal at first feared that some political retraction would be asked, but when assured that only his religious beliefs would be investigated, promptly submitted a statement which Father Obach says covered about the same ground as the earliest published of the retractions said to have been made on the eve of Rizal's death.

This document, inclosed with the priest's letter, was ready for the mail when Rizal came hurrying in to reclaim it. The marriage was off, for Mr. Taufer had taken his family and gone to Manila.

The explanation of this sudden departure was that, after the blind man had been told of the impossibility of anything being done for his eyes, he was informed of the proposed marriage. The trip had already cost him one daughter, he had found that his blindness was incurable, and now his only remaining daughter, who had for seventeen years been like his own child, was planning to leave him. He would have to return to Hongkong hopeless and accompanied only by a wife he had never seen, one who really was merely a servant. In his despair he said he had nothing to live for, and, seizing his razor, would have ended his life had not Rizal seized him just in time and held him, with the firm grasp his athletic training had given him, till the commandant came and calmed the excited blind man.

It resulted in Josefina returning to Manila with him, but after a while Mr Taufer listened to reason and she went back to Dapitan, after a short stay in Manila with Rizal's family, to whom she had carried his letter of introduction, taking considerable housekeeping furniture with her.

Further consideration changed Rizal's opinion as to marriage, possibly because the second time the priest may not have been so liberal in his requirements. The mother, too, seems to have suggested that as Spanish law had established civil marriage in the Philippines, and as the local government had not provided any way for people to avail themselves of the right, because the governor-general had pigeon-holed the royal decree, it would be less sinful for the two to consider themselves civilly married than for Rizal to do violence to his conscience by making any sort of political retraction. Any marriage so bought would be just as little a sacrament as an absolutely civil marriage, and the latter was free from hypocrisy.

So as man and wife Rizal and Josefina lived together in Talisay. Father Obach sought to prejudice public feeling in the town against the exile for the "scandal," though other scandals happenings with less reason were going on unrebuked. The pages of "Dapitan", which some have considered to be the first chapter of an unfinished novel, may reasonably be considered no more than Rizal's rejoinder to Father Obach, written in sarcastic vein and primarily for Carnicero's amusement, unless some date of writing earlier than this should hereafter be found for them.

Josefina was bright, vivacious, and a welcome addition to the little colony at Talisay, but at times Rizal had misgivings as to how it came that this foreigner should be permitted by a suspicious and absolute government to join him, when Filipinos, over whom the authorities could have exercised complete control, were kept away. Josefina's frequent visits to the convento once brought this suspicion to an open declaration of his misgivings by Rizal, but two days of weeping upon her part caused him to avoid the subiect thereafter. Could the exile have seen the confidential correspondence in the secret archives the plan would have been plain to him, for there it is suggested that his impressionable character could best be reached through the sufferings of his family, and that only his mother and sisters should be allowed to visit him. Steps in this plot were the gradual pardoning and returning of the members of his family to their homes.

Josefina must remain a mystery to us as she was to Rizal. While she was in a delicate condition Rizal played a prank on her, harmless in itself, which startled her so that she sprang forward and struck against an iron stand. Though it was pure accident and Rizal was scarcely at fault, he blamed himself for it, and his later devotion seems largely to have been trying to make amends.

The "burial of the son of Rizal," sometimes referred to as occurring at Dapitan, has for its foundation the consequences of this accident. A sketch hastily penciled in one of his medical books depicts an unusual condition apparent in the infant which, had it regularly made its appearance in the world some months later, would have been cherished by both parents; this loss was a great and common grief which banished thereafter all distrust upon his part and all occasion for it upon hers.

Rizal's mother and several of his sisters, the latter changing from time to time, had been present during this critical period. Another operation had been performed upon Mrs. Rizal's eyes, but she was restive and disregarded the ordinary precautions, and the son was in despair. A letter to his brother-inlaw, Manuel Hidalgo, who was inclined toward medical studies, says, "I now realize the reason why physicians are directed not to practice in their own families."

A story of his mother and Rizal, necessary to understand his peculiar attitude toward her, may serve as the transition from the hero's sad (later) married experience to the real romance of his life. Mrs. Rizal's talents commanded her son's admiration, as her care for him demanded his gratitude, but, despite the common opinion, he never had that sense of companionship with her that he enjoyed with his father. Mrs. Rizal was a strict disciplinarian and a woman of unexceptionable character, but she arrogated to herself an infallibility which at times was trying to those about her, and she foretold bitter fates for those who dared dispute her.

Just before José went abroad to study, while engaged to his cousin, Leonora Rivera, Mrs. Rivera and her daughter visited their relatives in Kalamba. Naturally the young man wished the guests to have the best of everything; one day when they visited a bathing place near by he used the family's newest carriage. Though this had not been forbidden, his mother spoke rather sharply about it; José ventured to remind her that guests were present and that it would be better to discuss the matter in private. Angry because one of her children ventured to dispute her, she replied: "You are an undutiful son. You will never accomplish anything which you undertake. All your plans will result in failure." These words could not be forgotten, as succeeding events seemed to make their prophecy come true, and there is pathos in one of Rizal's letters in which he reminds his mother that she had foretold his fate.

His thoughts of an early marriage were overruled because his unmarried sisters did not desire to have a sister-in-law in their home who would add to the household cares but was not trained to bear her share of them, and even Paciano, who was in his favor, thought that his younger brother would mar his career by marrying early.

So, with fervent promises and high hopes, Rizal had sailed away to make the fortune which should allow him to marry his cousin Leonora. She was constantly in his thoughts and his long letters were mailed with regular frequency during all his first years in Europe; but only a few of the earliest ever reached her, and as few replies came into his hands, though she was equally faithful as a correspondent.

Leonora's mother had been told that it was for the good of her daughter's soul and in the interest of her happiness that she should not become the wife of a man like Rizal, who was obnoxious to the Church and in disfavor with the government. So, by advice, Mrs. Rivera gradually withheld more and more of the correspondence upon both sides, until finally it ceased.

And she constantly suggested to the unhappy girl that her youthful lover had forgotten her amid the distractions and gayeties of Europe.

Then the same influence which had advised breaking off the correspondence found a person whom the mother and others joined in urging upon her as a husband, till at last, in the belief that she owed obedience to her mother, she reluctantly consented. Strangely like the proposed husband of the Maria Clara of "Noli Me Tangere," in which book Rizal had prophetically pictured her, this husband was "one whose children should rule "—an English engineer whose position had been found for him to make the match more desirable. Their marriage took place, and when Rizal returned to the Philippines she learned how she had been deceived. Then she asked for the letters that had been withheld, and when told that as a wife she might not keep love letters from any but her husband, she pleaded that they be burned and the ashes given her. This was done, and the silver box with the blackened bits of paper upon her dresser seemed to be a consolation during the few months of life which she knew would remain to her.

Another great disappointment to Rizal was the action of Despujol when he first arrived in
Dapitan, for he still believed in the GovernorGeneral's good faith and thought in that fertile but sparsely settled region he might plant his "New Kalamba" without the objection that had been urged against the British North Borneo project. All seemed to be going on favorably for the assembling of his relatives and neighbors in what then would be no longer exile, when most insultingly, the Governor-General refused the permission which Rizal had had reason to rely upon his granting. The exile was reminded of his deportation and taunted with trying to make himself a king. Though he did not know it, this was part of the plan which was to break his spirit, so that when he was touched with the sufferings of his family he would yield to the influences of his youth and make complete political retraction; thus would be removed the most reasonable, and therefore the most formidable, opponent of the unnatural conditions Philippines and of the selfish interests which were

profiting by them. But the plotters failed in their plan; they had mistaken their man.

During all this time Rizal had repeated chances to escape, and persons high in authority seem to have urged flight upon him. Running away, however, seemed to him a confession of guilt; the opportunities of doing so always unsettled him, for each time the battle of self-sacrifice had to be fought over again; but he remained firm in his purpose. To meet death bravely is one thing; to seek it is another and harder thing; but to refuse life and choose death over and over again during many years is the rarest kind of heroism.

Rizal used to make long trips, sometimes cruising for a week in his explorations of the Mindanao coast, and some of his friends proposed to charter a steamer in Singapore and, passing near Dapitan, pick him up on one of these trips. Another Philippine steamer going to Borneo suggested taking him on board as a rescue at sea and then landing him at their destination, where he would be free from Spanish power. Either of these schemes would have been feasible, but he refused both.

Plans, which materialized, to benefit the fishing industry by improved nets imported from his Laguna home, and to find a market for the abaka of Dapitan, were joined with the introduction of American machinery, for which Rizal acted as agent, among planters of neighboring islands. It was a busy, useful life, and in the economic advancement of his country the exile believed he was as patriotic as when he was working politically.

Rizal personally had been fortunate, for in company with the commandant and a Spaniard, originally deported for political reasons from the Peninsula, he had gained one of the richer prizes in the government lottery. These funds came most opportunely, for the land troubles and succeeding litigation had almost stripped the family of all its possessions. The account of the first news in Dapitan of the good fortune of the three is interestingly told in an official report to the Governor-General from the commandant. The official saw the infrequent mail steamer arriving with flying bunting and at once imagined some high authority was aboard; he hastened to the beach with a band of music to assist in the welcome, but was agreeably disappointed with the news of the luck which had befallen his prisoner and himself.

Not all of Dapitan life was profitable and prosperous. Yet in spite of this Rizal stayed in the town. This was pure self-sacrifice, for he refused to make any effort for his own release by invoking influences which could have brought pressure to bear upon the Spanish home government. He feared to act lest obstacles might be put in the way of the reforms that were apparently making headway through Despujol's initiative, and was content to wait rather than to jeopardize the prospects of others.

A plan for his transfer to the North, in the Ilokano country, had been deferred and had met with obstacles which Rizal believed were placed in its way through some of his own countrymen in the Peninsula who feared his influence upon the revenue with which politics was furnishing them.

Another proposal was to appoint Rizal district health officer for Dapitan, but this was merely a covert government bribe. While the exile expressed his willingness to accept the position, he did not make the "unequivocally Spanish" professions that were needed to secure this appointment.

Yet the government could have been satisfied of Rizal's innocence of any treasonable designs against Spain's sovereignty in the Islands had it known how the exile had declined an opportunity to head the movement which had been initiated on the eve of his deportation. His name had been used to gather the members together and his portrait hung in each Katipunan lodge hall, but all this was without Rizal's consent or even his knowledge.

The members, who had been paying
faithfully for four years, felt that it was time that something besides collecting money was done. Their restiveness and suspicions led Andrés Bonifacio, its head, to resort to Rizal, feeling that a word from the exile,

who had religiously held aloof from all politics since his deportation, would give the Katipunan leaders more time to mature their plans. So he sent a messenger to Dapitan, Pio Valenzuela, a doctor, who to conceal his mission took with him a blind man. Thus the doctor and his patient appeared as on a professional visit to the exiled oculist. But though the interview was successfully secured in this way, its results were far from satisfactory.

Far from feeling grateful for the consideration for the possible consequences to him which Valenzuela pretended had prompted the visit, Rizal indignantly insisted that the country came first. He cited the Spanish republics of South America, with their alternating revolutions and despotisms, as a warning against embarking on a change of government for which the people were not prepared. Education, he declared, was first necessary, and in his opinion general enlightenment was the only road to progress. Valenzuela cut short his trip, glad to escape without anyone realizing that Rizal and he had quarreled.

Bonifacio called Rizal a coward when he heard his emissary's report, and enjoined Valenzuela to say nothing of his trip. But the truth leaked out, and there was a falling away in Katipunan membership.

Doctor Rizal's own statement respecting the rebellion and Valenzuela's visit may fitly be quoted here:

"I had no notice at all of what was being planned until the first or second of July, in 1896, when Pio Valenzuela came to see me, saying that an uprising was being arranged. I told him that it was absurd, etc., etc., and he answered me that they could bear no more. I advised him that they should have patience, etc., etc. He added then that he had been sent because they had compassion on my life and that probably it would compromise me. I replied that they should have patience and that if anything happened to me I would then prove my innocence. 'Besides,' said I, 'don't consider me, but our country, which is the one that will suffer.' I went on to show how absurd was the movement.—This, later,

Pio Valenzuela testified.—He did not tell me that my name was being used, neither did he suggest that I was its chief, or anything of that sort.

"Those who testify that I am the chief (which I do not know, nor do I know of having ever treated with them), what proofs do they present of my having accepted this chiefship or that I was in relations with them or with their society? Either they have made use of my name for their own purposes or they have been deceived by others who have. Where is the chief who dictates no order and makes no arrangement, who is not consulted in anything about so important an enterprise until the last moment, and then when he decides against it is disobeyed? Since the seventh of July of 1892 I have entirely ceased political activity. It seems some have wished to avail themselves of my name for their own ends."

This was Rizal's second temptation to engage in politics, the first having been a trap laid by his enemies. A man had come to see Rizal in his earlier days in Dapitan, claiming to be a relative and seeking letters to prominent Filipinos. The deceit was too plain and Rizal denounced the envoy to the commandant, whose investigations speedily disclosed the source of the plot. Further prosecution, of course, ceased at once.

The visit of some image vendors from Laguna who never before had visited that region, and who seemed more intent on escaping notice than interested in business, appeared suspicious, but upon report of the Jesuits the matter was investigated and nothing really suspicious was found.

Rizal's charm of manner and attraction for every one he met is best shown by his relations with the successive commandants at Dapitan, all of whom, except Carnicero, were naturally predisposed against him, but every one became his friend and champion. One even asked relief on the ground of this growing favorable impression upon his part toward his prisoner.

At times there were rumors of Rizal's speedy pardon, and he would think of going regularly into scientific work, collecting for those European museums which had made him proposals that assured ample livelihood and congenial work.

Then Doctor Blumentritt wrote to him of the ravages of disease among the Spanish soldiers in Cuba and the scarcity of surgeons to attend them. Here was a labor "eminently humanitarian," to quote Rizal's words of his own profession, and it made so strong an appeal to him that, through the new governorgeneral, for Despujol had been replaced by Blanco, he volunteered his services. The minister of war of that time, General Azcarraga, was Philippine born. Blanco considered the time favorable for granting Rizal's petition and thus lifting the decree of deportation without the embarrassment of having the popular prisoner remain in the Islands.

The thought of resuming his travels evidently inspired the following poem, which was written at about this time. The translation is by Arthur P. Ferguson:

The Song of the Traveler

Like to a leaf that is fallen and withered,
Tossed by the tempest from pole unto pole; Thus roams the pilgrim abroad without purpose,
Roams without love, without country or soul.

Following anxiously treacherous fortune,
Fortune which e'en as he grasps at it flees; Vain though the hopes that his yearning is seeking,
Yet does the pilgrim embark on the seas!

Ever impelled by invisible power,
Destined to roam from the East to the West; Oft he remembers the faces of loved ones, Dreams of the day when he, too, was at rest.

Chance may assign him a tomb on the desert,
Grant him a final asylum of peace;

Soon by the world and his country forgotten, God rest his soul when his wanderings cease!

Often the sorrowful pilgrim is envied,
Circling the globe like a sea-gull above; Little, ah, little they know what a void Saddens his soul by the absence of love.

Home may the pilgrim return in the future, Back to his loved ones his footsteps he bends;

Naught will he find but the snow and the ruins,
Ashes of love and the tomb of his friends.

Pilgrim, begone! Nor return more hereafter.
Stranger thou art in the land of thy birth; Others may sing of their love while rejoicing,
Thou once again must roam o'er the earth.

Pilgrim, begone! Nor return more hereafter,
Dry are the tears that a while for thee ran;
Pilgrim, begone! And forget thy affliction, Loud laughs the world at the sorrows of man.

CHAPTER X

"Consummatum Est"

NOTICE of the granting of his request came to Rizal just when repeated disappointments had caused him to prepare for staying in Dapitan. Immediately he disposed of his salable possessions, including a Japanese tea set and large mirror now among the Rizal relics preserved by the government, and a piece of outlying land, the deed for which is also among the Rizalana in the Philippines library. Some half-finished busts were thrown into the pool behind the dam. Despite the short notice all was ready for the trip in time, and, attended by some of his schoolboys as well as by Josefina and Rizal's niece, the daughter of his youngest sister, Soledad, whom Josefina wished to adopt, the party set out for Manila.

The journey was not an uneventful one; at Dumaguete Rizal was the guest of a Spanish judge at dinner; in Cebu he operated successfully upon the eyes of a foreign merchant; and in Iloilo the local newspaper made much of his presence.

The steamer from Dapitan reached Manila a little too late for the mail boat for Spain, and Rizal obtained permission to await the next sailing on board the cruiser Castilla, in the bay. Here he was treated like a guest and more than once the Spanish captain invited members of Rizal's family to be his guests at dinner—Josefina with little Maria Luisa, the niece and the schoolboys, for whom positions had been obtained, in Manila.

The alleged uprising of the Katipunan occurred during this time. A Tondo curate, with an eye to promotion, professed to have discovered a gigantic conspiracy. Incited by him, the lower class of Spaniards in Manila made demonstrations against Blanco and tried to force that ordinarily sensible and humane executive into bloodthirsty measures, which should terrorize the Filipinos. Blanco had known of the Katipunan but realized that so long as interested parties were using it as a source of revenue, its activities would not go much beyond speechmaking. The rabble was not so far-seeing, and from high authorities came advice that the country was in a fever and could only be saved by blood-letting.

Wholesale arrests filled every possible place for prisoners in Manila. The guilt of one suspect consisted in having visited the American consul to secure the address of a New York medical journal, and other charges were just as frivolous. There was a reign of terror in Luzon and, to save themselves, members of the Katipunan resorted to that open warfare which, had Blanco's prudent counsels been regarded, would probably have been avoided.

While the excitement was at its height, with a number of executions failing to satisfy the blood-hunger, Rizal sailed for Spain, bearing letters of recommendation from Blanco. These vouched for his exemplary conduct during his exile and stated that he had in no way been implicated in the conspiracies then disturbing the Islands.

The Spanish mail boat upon which Rizal finally sailed had among its passengers a sick Jesuit, to whose care Rizal devoted himself, and though most of the passengers were openly hostile to one whom they supposed responsible for the existing outbreak, his professional skill led several to avail themselves of his services. These were given with a deference to the ship's doctor which made that official an admirer and champion of his colleague.

Three only of the passengers, however, were really friendly—one Juan Utor y Fernandez, a prominent Mason and republican, another exofficial in the Philippines who shared Utor's liberal views, and a young man whose father was republican.

But if Rizal's chief adversaries were content that he should go where he would not molest them or longer jeopardize their interests, the rabble that had been excited by the hired newspaper advocates was not so easily calmed. Every one who felt that his picture had been painted among the lower Spanish types portrayed in "Noli Me Tangere" was loud for revenge. The clamor grew so great that it seemed possible to take advantage of it to displace General Blanco, who was not a convenient tool for the interests.

So his promotion was bought, it is said, to get one Polavieja, a willing tool, in his place. As soon as this scheme was arranged, a cablegram ordering Rizal's arrest was sent; it overtook the steamer at Suez. Thus as a prisoner he completed his journey.

But this had not been entirely unforeseen, for when the steamer reached Singapore, Rizal's companion on board, the Filipino millionaire Pedro P. Roxas, had deserted the ship, urging the ex-exile to follow his example.

Rizal demurred, and said such flight would be considered confession of guilt, but he was not fully satisfied in his mind that he was safe. At each port of call his uncertainty as to what course to pursue manifested itself, for though he considered his duty to his country already done, and his life now his own, he would do nothing that suggested an uneasy conscience despite his lack of confidence in Spanish justice.

At first, not knowing the course of events in
Manila, he very naturally blamed GovernorGeneral Blanco for bad faith, and spoke rather harshly of him in a letter to Doctor Blumentritt, an opinion which he changed later when the truth was revealed to him in Manila.

Upon the arrival of the steamer in Barcelona the prisoner was transferred to Montjuich Castle, a political prison associated with many cruelties, there to await the sailing that very day of the Philippine mail boat. The Captain-General was the same Despujol who had decoyed Rizal into the power of the Spaniards four years before. An interesting interview of some hours' duration took place between the governor and the prisoner, in which the clear conscience of the latter seems to have stirred some sense of shame in the man who had so dishonorably deceived him.

He never heard of the effort of London friends to deliver him at Singapore by means of habeas-corpus proceedings. Mr. Regidor furnished the legal inspiration and Mr. Baustead the funds for getting an opinion as to Rizal's status as a prisoner when in British waters, from Sir Edward Clarke, ex-solicitorgeneral of Great Britain. Captain Camus, a Filipino living in Singapore, was cabled to, money was made available in the Chartered Bank of Singapore, as Mr. Baustead's father's firm was in business in that city, and a lawyer, now Sir Hugh Fort, K.C., of London, was retained. Secretly, in order that the attempt, if unsuccessful, might not jeopardize the prisoner, a petition was presented to the Supreme Court of the Straits Settlements reciting the facts that Doctor José Rizal, according to the Philippine practice of punishing Freemasons without trial, was being deprived of his liberty without warrant of law upon a ship then within the jurisdiction of the court.

According to Spanish law Rizal was being illegally held on the Spanish mail steamer Colon, for the Constitution of Spain forbade detention except on a judge's order, but like most Spanish laws the Constitution was not much respected by Spanish officials. Rizal had never had a hearing before any judge, nor had any charge yet been placed against him. The writ of habeas corpus was justified, provided the Colon were a merchant ship that would be subject to British law when in British port, but the mail steamer that carried Rizal also had on board Spanish soldiers and flew the royal flag as if it were a national transport. No one was willing to deny that this condition made the ship floating Spanish territory, and the judge declined to issue the writ.

Rizal reached Manila on November 3 and was at once transferred to Fort Santiago, at first being held in a dungeon "incomunicado" and later occupying a small cell on the ground floor. Its furnishings had to be supplied by himself and they consisted of a small rattan table, a highbacked chair, a steamer chair of the same material, and a cot of the kind used by Spanish officers—canvas top and collapsible frame which closed up lengthwise. His meals were sent in by his family, being carried by one of his former pupils at Dapitan, and such cooking or heating as was necessary was done on an alcohol lamp which had been presented to him in Paris by Mrs. Tavera.

An unsuccessful effort had been made earlier to get evidence against Rizal by torturing his brother Paciano. For hours the elder brother had been seated at a table in the headquarters of the political police, a thumbscrew on one hand and pen in the other, while before him was a confession which would implicate José Rizal in the Katipunan uprising. The paper remained unsigned, though Paciano was hung up by the elbows till he was insensible, and then cut down that the fall might revive him. Three days of this maltreatment made him so ill that there was no possibility of his signing anything, and he was carted home.

It would not be strictly accurate to say that at the close of the nineteenth century the Spaniards of Manila were using the same tortures that had made their name abhorrent in Europe three centuries earlier, for there was some progress; electricity was employed at times as an improved method of causing anguish, and the thumbscrews were much more neatly finished than those used by the Dons of the Dark Ages.

Rizal did not approve of the rebellion and desired to issue a manifesto to those of his countrymen who had been deceived into believing that he was their leader. But the proclamation was not politic, for it contained none of those fulsomely flattering phrases which passed for patriotism in the feverish days of 1896. The address was not allowed to be made public but it was passed on to the prosecutor to form another count in the indictment of José Rizal for not esteeming Spanish civilization.

The following address to some Filipinos shows more clearly and unmistakably than any words of mine exactly what was the state of Rizal's mind in this matter.

COUNTRYMEN:

On my return from Spain I learned that my name had been in use, among some who were in arms, as a war-cry. The news came as a painful surprise, but, believing it already closed, I kept silent over an incident which I considered irremediable. Now I notice indications of the disturbances continuing and if any still, in good or bad faith, are availing themselves of my name, to stop this abuse and undeceive the unwary I hasten to address you these lines that the truth may be known.

From the very beginning, when I first had notice of what was being planned, I opposed it, fought it, and demonstrated its absolute impossibility. This is the fact, and witnesses to my words are now living. I was convinced that the scheme was utterly absurd, and, what was worse, would bring great suffering.

I did even more. When later, against my advice, the movement materialized, of my own accord I offered not alone my good offices, but my very life, and even my name, to be used in whatever way might seem best, toward stifling the rebellion; for, convinced of the ills which it would bring, I considered myself fortunate if, at any sacrifice, I could prevent such useless misfortunes. This equally is of record. My countrymen, I have given proofs that I am one most anxious for liberties for our country, and I am still desirous of them. But I place as a prior condition the education of the people, that by means of instruction and industry our country may have an individuality of its own and make itself worthy of these liberties. I have recommended in my writings the study of the civic virtues, without which there is no redemption. I have written likewise (and I repeat my words) that reforms, to be beneficial, must come from above, that those which come from below are irregularly gained and uncertain.

Holding these ideas, I cannot do less than condemn, and I do condemn this uprising—as absurd, savage, and plotted behind my back —which dishonors us Filipinos and discredits those who could plead our cause. I abhor its criminal methods and disclaim all part in it, pitying from the bottom of my heart the unwary who have been deceived.

Return, then, to your homes, and may God pardon those who have worked in bad faith!

José Rizal.

Fort Santiago, December 15, 1896.

Finally a court-martial was convened for Rizal's trial, in the Cuartel de España. No trained counsel was allowed to defend him, but a list of young army officers was presented from which he might select a nominal defender. Among the names was one which was familiar, Luis Taviel de Andrade, and he proved to be the brother of Rizal's companion during his visit to the Philippines in 1887-88. The young man did his best and risked unpopularity in order to be loyal to his client. His defense reads pitiably weak in these days but it was risky then to say even so much.

The judge advocate in a ridiculously bombastic effusion gave an alleged sketch of Rizal's life which showed ignorance of almost every material event, and then formulated the first precise charge against the prisoner, which was that he had founded an illegal society, alleging that the Liga Filipina had for its sole object to commit the crime of rebellion.

The second charge was that Rizal was responsible for the existing rebellion, having caused it, bringing it on by his unceasing labors. An aggravating circumstance was found in the prisoner's being a native of the Philippines.

The penalty of death was asked of the court, and in the event of pardon being granted by the crown, the prisoner should at least remain under surveillance for the rest of his life and pay as damages 20,000 pesos.

The arguments are so absurd, the bias of the court so palpable, that it is not worth while to discuss them. The parallel proceedings in the military trial and execution of Francisco Ferret in Barcelona in 1909 caused worldwide indignation, and the illegality of almost every step, according to Spanish law, was shown in numerous articles in the European and American press. Rizal's case was even more brazenly unfair, but Manila was too remote and the news too carefully censored for the facts to become known.

The prisoner's arms were tied, corded from elbow to elbow behind his back, and thus he sat through the weary trial while the public jeered him and clamored for his condemnation as the bloodthirsty crowds jeered and clamored in the French Reign of terror.

Then came the verdict and the prisoner was invited to acknowledge the regularity of the proceedings in the farcical trial by signing the record. To this Rizal demurred, but after a vain protest, affixed his signature.

He was at once transferred to the Fort chapel, there to pass the last twenty-four hours of his life in preparing for death. The military chaplain offered his services, which were courteously declined, but when the Jesuits came, those instructors of his youth were eagerly welcomed.

Rizal's trial had awakened great interest and accounts of everything about the prisoner were cabled by eager correspondents to the Madrid newspapers. One of the newspaper men who visited Rizal in his cell mentions the courtesy of his reception, and relates how the prisoner played the host and insisted on showing his visitor those attentions which Spanish politeness considers due to a guest, saying that these must be permitted, for he was in his own home. The interviewer found the prisoner perfectly calm and natural, serious of course, but not at all overwhelmed by the near prospect of death, and in discussing his career Rizal displayed that dispassionate attitude toward his own doings that was characteristic of him. Almost as though speaking of a stranger he mentioned that if Archbishop Nozaleda's sane view had been taken and "Noli Me Tangere" not preached against, he would not have been in prison, and perhaps the rebellion would never have occurred. It is easy for us to recognize that the author referred to the misconception of his novel, which had arisen from the publication of the censor's extracts, which consisted of whatever could be construed into coming under one of the three headings of attacks on religion, attacks on government, and reflections on Spanish character, without the slightest regard to the context.

But the interviewer, quite honestly, reported Rizal to be regretting his novel instead of regretting its miscomprehension, and he seems to have been equally in error in the way he mistook Rizal's meaning about the republicans in Spain having led him astray. Rizal's exact words are not given in the newspaper account, but it is not likely that a man would make admissions in a newspaper interview, which if made formally, would have saved his life. Rizal's memory has one safeguard against the misrepresentations which the absence of any witnesses favorable to him make possible regarding his last moments: a political retraction would have prevented his execution, and since the execution did take place, it is reasonable to believe that Rizal died holding the views for which he had expressed himself willing to suffer martyrdom.

Yet this view does not reflect upon the good faith of the reporter. It is probable that the prisoner was calling attention to the illogical result that, though he had disregarded the advice of the radical Spaniards who urged him to violent measures, his peaceable agitation had been misunderstood and brought him to the same situation as though he had actually headed a rebellion by arms. His slighting opinion of his great novel was the view he had always held, for like all men who do really great things, he was the reverse of a braggart, and in his remark that he had attempted to do great things without the capacity for gaining success, one recognizes his remembrance of his mother's angry prophecy foretelling failure in all he undertook.

His family waited long outside the Governor-
General's place to ask a pardon, but in vain; General Polavieja had to pay the price of his appointment and refused to see them.

The mother and sisters, however, were permitted to say farewell to Rizal in the chapel, under the eyes of the death-watch. The prisoner had been given the unusual privilege of not being tied, but he was not allowed to approach near his relatives, really for fear that he might pass some writing to them—the pretext was made that Rizal might thus obtain the means for committing suicide.

To his sister Trinidad Rizal spoke of having nothing to give her by way of remembrance except the alcohol cooking lamp which he had been using, a gift, as he mentioned, from Mrs. Tavera. Then he added quickly, in English, so that the listening guard would not understand, "There is something inside."

The other events of Rizal's last twenty-four hours, for he went in to the chapel at seven in the morning of the day preceding his execution, are perplexing. What purported to be a detailed account was promptly published in Barcelona, on Jesuit authority, but one must not forget that Spaniards are not of the phlegmatic disposition which makes for accuracy in minute matters and even when writing history they are dramatically ificlined. So while the truthfulness, that is the intent to be fair, may not be questioned, it would not be strange if those who wrote of what happened in the chapel in Fort Santiago during Rizal's last hours did not escape entirely from the influence of the national characteristics. In the main their narrative is to be accepted, but the possibility of unconscious coloring should not be disregarded. In substance it is alleged that Rizal greeted

his old instructors and other past acquaintances in a friendly way. He asked for copies of the Gospels and the writings of Thomas-à-Kempis, desired to be formally married to Josefina, and asked to be allowed to confess. The Jesuits responded that first it would be necessary to investigate how far his beliefs conformed to the Roman Catholic teachings. Their catechizing convinced them that he was not orthodox and a religious debate ensued in which Rizal, after advancing all known arguments, was completely vanquished. His marriage was made contingent upon his signing a retraction of his published heresies.

The Archbishop had prepared a form which the Jesuits believed Rizal would be little likely to sign, and they secured permission to substitute a shorter one of their own which included only the absolute essentials for reconciliation with the Church, and avoided all political references. They say that Rizal objected only to a disavowal of Freemasonry, stating that in England, where he held his membership, the Masonic institution was not hostile to the Church. After some argument, he waived this point and wrote out, at a Jesuit's dictation, the needed retraction, adding some words to strengthen it in parts, indicating his Catholic education and that the act was of his own free will and accord.

The prisoner, the priests, and all the Spanish officials present knelt at the altar, at Rizal's suggestion, while he read his retraction aloud. Afterwards he put on a blue scapular, kissed the image of the Sacred Heart he had carved years before, heard mass as when a student in the Ateneo, took communion, and read his àKempis or prayed in the intervals. He took breakfast with the Spanish officers, who now regarded him very differently. At six Josefina entered and was married to him by Father Balanguer.

Now in this narrative there are some apparent discrepancies. Mention is made of Rizal having in an access of devotion signed in a devotionary all the acts of faith, and it is said that this book was given to one of his sisters. His chapel gifts to his family have been examined, but though there is a book of devotion, "The Anchor of Faith," it contains no other signature than the presentation on a flyleaf. As to the religious controversy: while in Dapitan Rizal carried on with Father Pio Pi, the Jesuit superior, a lengthy discussion involving the interchange of many letters, but he succeeded in fairly maintaining his views, and these views would hardly have caused him to be called Protestant in the Roman Catholic churches of America. Then the theatrical reading aloud of his retraction before the altar does not conform to Rizal's known character. As to the anti-Masonic arguments, these appear to be from a work by Monsignor Dupanloup and therefore were not new to Rizal; furthermore, the book was in his own library.

Again, it seems strange that Rizal should have asserted that his Masonic membership was in London when in visiting St. John's Lodge, Scotch Constitution, in Hongkong in November of 1891, since which date he had not been in London, he registered as from "Temple du honneur de les amis français," an old-established Paris lodge.

Also the sister Lucia, who was said to have been a witness of the marriage, is not positive that it occurred, having only seen the priest at the altar in his vestments. The record of the marriage has been stated to be in the Manila Cathedral, but it is not there, and as the Jesuit in officiating would have been representing the military chaplain, the entry should have been in the Fort register, now in Madrid. Rizal's burial, too, does not indicate that he died in the faith, yet it with the marriage has been used as an argument for proving that the retraction must have been made.

The retraction itself appears in two versions, with slight differences. No one outside the Spanish faction has ever seen the original, though the family nearly got into trouble by their persistence in trying to get sight of it after its first publication.

The foregoing might suggest some disbelief, but in fact they are only proofs of the remarks already made about the Spanish carelessness in details and liking for the dramatic.

The writer believes Rizal made a retraction, was married canonically, and was given what was intended to be Christian burial.

The grounds for this belief rest upon the fact that he seems never to have been estranged in faith from the Roman Catholic Church, but he objected only to certain political and mercenary abuses. The first retraction is written in his style and it certainly contains nothing he could not have signed in Dapitan. In fact, Father Obach says that when he wanted to marry Josefina on her first arrival there, Rizal prepared a practically similar statement. Possibly the report of that priest aided in outlining the draft which the Jesuits substituted for the Archbishop's form. There is no mention of evasions or mental reservations and Rizal's renunciation of Masonry might have been qualified by the quibble that it was "the Masonry which was an enemy of the Church" that he was renouncing. Then since his association (not affiliation) had been with Masons not hostile to religion, he was not abandoning these.

The possibility of this line of thought having suggested itself to him appears in his evasions on the witness-stand at his trial. Though he answered with absolute frankness whatever concerned himself and in everyday life was almost quixotically truthful, when cross-examined about others who would be jeopardized by admitting his acquaintance with them, he used the subterfuge of the symbolic names of his Masonic acquaintances. Thus he would say, "I know no one by that name," since care was always taken to employ the symbolic names in introductions and conversations.

Rizal's own symbolic name was "Dimas Alang"—Tagalog for "Noli Me Tangere"— and his nom de plume in some of his controversial publications. The use of that name by one of his companions on the railroad trip to Tarlac entirely mystified a station master, as appears in the secret report of the espionage of that trip, which just preceded his deportation to Dapitan. Another possible explanation is that, since Freemasonry professes not to disturb the duties which its members owe to God, their country or their families, he may have considered himself as a good Mason under obligation to do whatever was demanded by these superior interests, all three of which were at this time involved.

The argument that it was his pride that restrained him suggested to Rizal the possibility of his being unconsciously under an influence which during his whole life he had been combating, and he may have considered that his duty toward God required the sacrifice of this pride.

For his country his sacrifice would have been blemished were any religious stigma to attach to it. He himself had always been careful of his own good name, and as we have said elsewhere, he told his companions that in their country's cause whatever they offered on the altars of patriotism must be as spotless as the sacrificial lambs of Levitical law.

Furthermore, his work for a tranquil future for his family would be unfulfilled were he to die outside the Church. Josefina's anomalous status, justifiable when all the facts were known, would be sure to bring criticism upon her unless corrected by the better defined position of a wife by a church marriage. Then the aged parents and the numerous children of his sisters would by his act be saved the scandal that in a country so mediævally pious as the Philippines would come from having their relative die "an unrepentant heretic."

Rizal had received from the Jesuits, while in prison, several religious books and pictures, which he used as remembrances for members of his family, writing brief dedications upon them. Then he said good-by to Josefina, asking in a low voice some question to which she answered in English, "Yes, yes," and aloud inquiring how she would be able to gain a living, since all his property had been seized by the Spanish government to satisfy the 20,000 pesetas costs which was included in the sentence of death against him. Her reply was that she could earn money giving lessons in English.

The journey from the Fort to the place of execution, then Bagumbayan Field, now called the Luneta, was on foot. His arms were tied tightly behind his back, and he was surrounded by a heavy guard. The Jesuits accompanied him and some of his Dapitan schoolboys were in the crowd, while one friendly voice, that of a Scotch merchant still resident in Manila, called out in English, "Good-by, Rizal."

The route was along the Malecon Drive where as a college student he had walked with his fiancée, Leonora. Above the city walls showed the twin towers of the Ateneo, and when he asked about them, for they were not there in his boyhood days, he spoke of the happy years that he had spent in the old school. The beauty of the morning, too, appealed to him, and may have recalled an experience of his '87 visit when he said to a friend whom he met on the beach during an early morning walk: "Do you know that I have a sort of foreboding that some such sunshiny morning as this I shall be out here facing a firing squad?"

Troops held back the crowds and left a large square for the tragedy, while artillery behind them was ready for suppressing any attempt at rescuing the prisoner. None came, however, for though Rizal's brother Paciano had joined the insurrectionary forces in Cavite when the death sentence showed there was no more hope for José, he had discouraged the demonstration that had been planned as soon as he learned how scantily the insurgents were armed, hardly a score of serviceable firearms being in the possession of their entire "army."

The firing squad was of Filipino soldiers, while behind them, better armed, were Spaniards in case these tried to evade the fratricidal part assigned them. Rizal's composure aroused the curiosity of a Spanish military surgeon standing by and he asked, "Colleague, may I feel your pulse?" Without other reply the prisoner twisted one of his hands as far from his body as the cords which bound him allowed, so that the other doctor could place his fingers on the wrist. The beats were steady and showed neither excitement nor fear, was the report made later.

His request to be allowed to face his executioners was denied as being out of the power of the commanding officer to grant, though Rizal declared that he did not deserve such a death, for he was no traitor to Spain. It was promised, however, that his head should be respected, and as unblindfolded and erect Rizal turned his back to receive their bullets, he twisted a hand to indicate under the shoulder where the soldiers should aim so as to reach his heart. Then as the volley came, with a last supreme effort of will power, he turned and fell face upwards, thus receiving the subsequent "shots of grace" which ended his life, so that in form as well as fact he did not die a traitor's death.

The Spanish national air was played, that march of Cadiz which should have recalled a violated constitution, for by the laws of Spain itself Rizal was illegally executed.

Vivas, laughter and applause were heard, for it had been the social event of the day, with breakfasting parties on the walls and on the carriages, full of interested onlookers of both sexes, lined up conveniently near for the sightseeing.

The troops defiled past the dead body, as though reviewed by it, for the most commanding figure of all was that which lay lifeless, but the center of all eyes. An officer, realizing the decency due to death, drew his handkerchief from the dead man's pocket and spread the silk over the calm face. A crimson stain soon marked the whiteness emblematic of the pure life that had just ended, and with the glorious blue overhead, the tricolor of Liberty, which had just claimed another martyr, was revealed in its richest beauty.

Sir Hugh Clifford (now Governor of Ceylon), in Blackwood's Magazine, "The Story of José Rizal, the Filipino; A

Fragment of Recent Asiatic History," comments as follows on the disgraceful doing of that day:

"It was," he writes, "early morning, December 30, 1896, and the bright sunshine of the tropics streamed down upon the open space, casting hard fantastic shadows, and drenching with its splendor two crowds of sightseers. The one was composed of Filipinos, cowed, melancholy, sullen, gazing through hopeless eyes at the final scene in the life of their great countryman—the man who had dared to champion their cause, and to tell the world the story of their miseries; the other was blithe of air, gay with the uniforms of officers and the bright dresses of Spanish ladies, the men jesting and laughing, the women shamelessly applauding with waving handkerchiefs and clapping palms, all alike triumphing openly in the death of the hated 'Indian,' the 'brother of the waterbuffalo,' whose insolence had wounded their pride.

* * * Turning away, sick at heart, from thecontemplation of this bitter tragedy, it is with a thrill of almost vindictive satisfaction that one remembers that less than eighteen months later the Luneta echoed once more to the sound of a mightier fusillade—the roar of the great guns with which the battle of Manila Bay was fought and won.

* * * And if in the moment of his lastsupreme agony the power to probe the future had been vouchsafed to José Rizal, would he not have died happy in the knowledge that the land he loved so dearly was very soon to be transferred into such safekeeping?"

CHAPTER XI

The After-Life in Memory

An hour or so after the shooting a deadwagon from San Juan de Diós Hospital took Rizal's body to Paco Cemetery. The civil governor of Manila was in charge and there also were present the members of a Church society whose duty it was to attend executions.

Rizal had been wearing a black suit which he had obtained for his European trip, and a derby hat, not only appropriate for a funeral occasion because of their somber color, but also more desirable than white both for the full day's wear, since they had to be put on before the twenty-four hours in the chapel, and for the lying on the ground which would follow the execution of the sentence. A plain box inclosed the remains thus dressed, for even the hat was picked up and encoffined.

No visitors were admitted to the cemetery while the interment was going on, and for several weeks after guards watched over the grave, lest Filipinos might come by night to steal away the body and apportion the clothing among themselves as relics of a martyr. Even the exact spot of the interment was intended to be unknown, but friends of the family were among the attendants at the burial and dropped into the grave a marble slab which had been furnished them, bearing the initials of the full baptismal name, José Protasio Rizal, in reversed order.

The entry of the burial, like that of three of his followers of the Liga Filipina who were among the dozen executed a fortnight later, was on the back flyleaf of the cemetery register, with three or four words of explanation later erased and now unknown. On the previous page was the entry of a suicide's death, and following it is that of the British Consul who died on the eve of
Manila's surrender and whose body, by the
Archbishop's permission, was stored in a
Paco niche till it could be removed to the Protestant (foreigners') cemetery at San Pedro Macati.

The day of Rizal's execution, the day of his birth and the day of his first leaving his native land was a Wednesday. All that night, and the next day, the celebration continued the volunteers, who were particularly responsible, like their fellows in Cuba, for the atrocities which disgraced Spain's rule in the Philippines, being especially in evidence. It was their clamor that had made the bringing back of Rizal possible, their demands for his death had been most prominent in his socalled trial, and now they were praising themselves for their "patriotism." The landlords had objected to having their land titles questioned and their taxes raised. The other friar orders, as well as these, were opposed to a campaign which sought their transfer from profitable parishes to selfsacrificing missionary labors. But probably none of them as organizations desired Rizal's death.

Rizal's old teachers wished for the restoration of their former pupil to the faith of his childhood, from which they believed he had departed. Through Despujol they seem to have worked for an opportunity for influencing him, yet his death was certainly not in their plans.

Some Filipinos, to save themselves, tried to complicate Rizal with the Katipunan uprising by palpable falsehoods. But not every man is heroic and these can hardly be blamed, for if all the alleged confessions were not secured by actual torture, they were made through fear of it, since in 1896 there was in Manila the legal practice of causing bodily suffering by mediæval methods supplemented by torments devised by modern science.

Among the Spaniards in Manila then, reënforced by those whom the uprising had frightened out of the provinces, were a few who realized that they belonged among the classes caricatured in Rizal's novels—some incompetent, others dishonest, cruel ones, the illiterate, wretched specimens that had married outside their race to get money and find wives who would not know them for what they were, or drunken husbands of viragoes. They came to the Philippines because they were below the standard of their homeland. These talked the loudest and thus dominated the undisciplined volunteers. With nothing divine about them, since they had not forgotten, they did not forgive. So when the Tondo "discoverer" of the Katipunan fancied he saw opportunity for promotion in fanning their flame of wrath, they claimed their victims, and neither the panic-stricken populace nor the weak-kneed government could withstand them.

Once more it must be repeated that Spain has no monopoly of bad characters, nor suffers in the comparison of her honorable citizenship with that of other nationalities, but her system in the Philippines permitted abuses which good governments seek to avoid or, in the rare occasions when this is impossible, aim to punish. Here was the Spanish shortcoming, for these were the defects which made possible so strange a story as this biography unfolds. "José Rizal," said a recent Spanish writer, "was the living indictment of Spain's wretched colonial system."

Rizal's family were scattered among the homes of friends brave enough to risk the popular resentment against everyone in any way identified with the victim of their prejudice.

As New Year's eve approached, the bands ceased playing and the marchers stopped parading. Their enthusiasm had worn itself out in the two continuous days of celebration, and there was a lessening of the hospitality with which these "heroes" who had "saved the fatherland" at first had been entertained. Their great day of the year became of more interest than further remembrance of the bloody occurrence on Bagumbayan Field. To those who mourned a son and a brother the change must have come as a welcome relief, for even sorrow has its degrees, and the exultation over the death embittered their grief.

To the remote and humble home where Rizal's widow and the sister to whom he had promised a parting gift were sheltered, the Dapitan schoolboy who had attended his imprisoned teacher brought an alcohol cooking-lamp. It was midnight before they dared seek the "something" which Rizal had said was inside. The alcohol was emptied from the tank and, with a convenient hairpin, a tightly folded and doubled piece of paper was dislodged from where it had been wedged in, out of sight, so that its rattling might not betray it.

It was a single sheet of notepaper bearing verses in Rizal's well-known handwriting and familiar style. Hastily the young boy copied them, making some minor mistakes owing to his agitation and unfamiliarity with the language, and the copy, without explanation, was mailed to Mr.

Basa in Hongkong. Then the original was taken by the two women with their few possessions and they fled to join the insurgents in Cavite.

The following translation of these verses was made
by Charles Derbyshire:

My Last Farewell

Farewell, dear Fatherland, clime of the sun caress'd,
Pearl of the Orient seas, our Eden lost! Gladly now I go to give thee this faded life's best,
And were it brighter, fresher, or more blest, Still would I give it thee, nor count the cost.

On the field of battle, 'mid the frenzy of fight,

Others have given their lives, without doubt or heed;
The place matters not—cypress or laurel or lily white,
Scaffold of open plain, combat or martyrdom's plight, 'Tis ever the same, to serve our home and country's need.

I die just when I see the dawn break, Through the gloom of night, to herald the day;
And if color is lacking my blood thou shalt take,
Pour'd out at need for thy dear sake, To dye with its crimson the waking ray.

My dreams, when life first opened to me, My dreams, when the hopes of youth beat high,
Were to see thy lov'd face, O gem of the
Orient sea,
From gloom and grief, from care and sorrow free;

No blush on thy brow, no tear in thine eye Dream of my life, my living and burning desire,
All hail! cries the soul that is now to take flight;

All hail! And sweet it is for thee to expire; To die for thy sake, that thou mayst aspire; And sleep in thy bosom eternity's long night.

If over my grave some day thou seest grow,
In the grassy sod, a humble flower,
Draw it to thy lips and kiss my soul so, While I may feel on my brow in the cold tomb below
The touch of thy tenderness, thy breath's warm power.

Let the moon beam over me soft and serene, Let the dawn shed over me its radiant flashes,
Let the wind with sad lament over me keen;
And if on my cross a bird should be seen, Let it trill there its hymn of peace to my ashes.

Let the sun draw the vapors up to the sky,
And heavenward in purity bear my tardy protest;
Let some kind soul o'er my untimely fate sigh,
And in the still evening a prayer be lifted on high
From thee, O my country, that in God I may rest.

Pray for all those that hapless have died, For all who have suffered the unmeasur'd pain;
For our mothers that bitterly their woes have cried,
For widows and orphans, for captives by torture tried;
And then for thyself that redemption thou mayst gain.

And when the dark night wraps the graveyard around,
With only the dead in their vigil to see; Break not my repose or the mystery profound,
And perchance thou mayst hear a sad hymn resound;
'Tis I, O my country, raising a song unto thee.

When even my grave is remembered no more,
Unmark'd by never a cross nor a stone; Let the plow sweep through it, the spade turn it o'er,

That my ashes may carpet thy earthly floor,   Before into nothingness at last they are blown.

Then will oblivion bring to me no care,
As over thy vales and plains I sweep;
Throbbing and cleansed in thy space and air,   With color and light, with song and lament I fare,
Ever repeating the faith that I keep.

My Fatherland ador'd, that sadness to my sorrow lends,
Beloved Filipinas, hear now my last goodby!
I give thee all: parents and kindred and friends;
For I go where no slave before the oppressor bends,

Where faith can never kill, and God reigns e'er on high!

Farewell to you all, from my soul torn away,   Friends of my childhood in the home dispossessed!
Give thanks that I rest from the wearisome day!
Farewell to thee, too, sweet friend that lightened my way;
Beloved creatures all, farewell! In death there is rest!

For some time such belongings of Rizal as had been intrusted to Josefina had been in the care of the American Consul in Manila for as the adopted daughter of the American Taufer she had claimed his protection. Stories are told of her as a second Joan of Arc, but it is not likely that one of the few rifles which the insurgents had would be turned over to a woman. After a short experience in the field, much of it spent in nursing her sister-in-law through a fever, Mrs. Rizal returned to Manila. Then came a brief interview with the

Governor-General. He had learned that his "administrative powers" to exile without trial did not extend to foreigners, but by advice of her consul she soon sailed for Hongkong.

Mrs. Rizal at first lived in the Basa home and received considerable attention from the Filipino colony. There was too great a difference between the freedom accorded Englishwomen and the restraints surrounding Spanish ladies however, to avoid difficulties and misunderstandings, for very long. She returned to her adopted father's house and after his death married Vicente Abad, a Cebuan, son of a Spaniard who had been prominent in the Tabacalera Company and had become an agent of theirs in Hongkong after he had completed his studies there.

Two weeks after Rizal's execution a dozen other members of his "Liga Filipina" were executed on the Luneta. One was a millionaire, Francisco Roxas, who had lost his mind, and believing that he was in church, calmly spread his handkerchief on the ground and knelt upon it as had been his custom in childhood. An old man, Moises Salvador, had been crippled by torture so that he could not stand and had to be laid upon the grass to be shot. The others met their death standing.

That bravery and cruelty do not usually go together was amply demonstrated in Polavieja's case and by the volunteers. The latter once showed their patriotism, after a banquet, by going to the water's edge on the Luneta and firing volleys at the insurgents across the bay, miles away. The General was relieved of his command after he had fortified a camp with siege guns against the boloarmed insurgents, who, however, by captures from the Spaniards were gradually becoming better equipped. But he did not escape condemnation from his own countrymen, and when he visited Giron, years after he had returned to the Peninsula, circulars were distributed among the crowd, bearing Rizal's last verses, his portrait, and the charge that to Polavieja was due the loss of the Philippines to Spain.

The Katipunan insurgents in time were bought off by General Primo de Rivera, once more returned to the Islands for further plunder. The money question does not concern Rizal's life, but his prediction of suffering to the country came true, for while the leaders with the first payment and hostages for their own safety sailed away to live securely in

Hongkong, the poorer people who remained suffered the vengeance of a government which seems never to have kept a promise to its people. Whether reforms were pledged is disputed, but if any were, they never were put into effect. No more money was paid, and the first instalment, preserved by the prudent leaders, equipped them when, owing to Dewey's victory, they were enabled to return to their country.

On the first anniversary of Rizal's execution some Spaniards desecrated the grave, while on one of the niches, rented for the purpose, many feet away, the family hung wreaths with Tagalog dedications but no name.

August 13, 1898, the Spanish flag came down from Fort Santiago in evidence of the surrender of the city. At the first opportunity Paco Cemetery was visited and Rizal's body raised for a more decent interment. Vainly his shoes were searched for a last message which he had said might be concealed there, for the dampness had made any paper unrecognizable. Then a simple cross was erected, resting on a marble block carved, as had been the smaller one which secretly had first marked the spot, with the reversed initials "R. P. J."

The first issue of a Filipino newspaper under the new government was entirely dedicated to Rizal. The second anniversary of his execution was observed with general unanimity, his countrymen demonstrating that those who were seeing the dawn of the new day were not forgetful of the greatest of those who had fallen in the night, to paraphrase his own words.

His widow returned and did live by giving lessons in English, at first privately in Cebu, where one of her pupils was the present and first Speaker of the Philippine Assembly, and afterwards as a government employee in the public schools and in the "Liceo" of Manila.

With the establishment of civil government a new province was formed near Manila, including the land across the lake to which, as a lad in Kalamba, Rizal had often wonderingly looked, and the name of Rizal Province was given it.

Later when public holidays were provided for by the new laws, the anniversary of Rizal's execution was in the list, and it has become the great day of the year, with the entire community uniting, for Spaniards no longer consider him to have been a traitor to Spain and the American authorities have founded a government in conformity with his teachings.

On one of these occasions, December 30,
1905, William Jennings Bryan, "The Great American Commoner," gave the Rizal Day address, in the course of which he said:

"If you will permit me to draw one lesson from the life of Rizal, I will say that he presents an example of a great man consecrated to his country's welfare. He, though dead, is a living rebuke to the scholar who selfishly enjoys the privilege of an ample education and does not impart the benefits of it to his fellows. His example is worth much to the people of these Islands, to the child who reads of him, to the young and old."

The fiftieth anniversary of Rizal's birth was observed throughout the Archipelago with exercises in every community by public schools now organized along the lines he wished, to make self-dependent, capable men and women, strong in body as in mind, knowing and claiming their own rights, and recognizing and respecting those of others.

His father died early in the year that the flags changed, but the mother lived to see honor done her son and to prove herself as worthy, for when the Philippine Legislature wanted to set aside a considerable sum for her use, she declined it with the true and rightfully proud assertion, that her family had never been patriotic for money. Her funeral, in 1911, was an occasion of public mourning, the Governor-General, Legislature and chief men of the Islands attending, and all public business being suspended by proclamation for the day.

A capitol for the representatives of the free people of the Philippines, and worthy of the pioneer democratic government in the Orient, is soon to be erected on the Luneta, facing the big Rizal monument which will mark the place of execution of the man who gave his life to prepare his countrymen for the changed conditions.

CPSIA information can be obtained
at www.ICGtesting.com
Printed in the USA
LVHW091121041119
636250LV00004B/960/P